CHARADE

LISA MARIE RICE

OLIVER-HEBER BOOKS

PUBLISHER'S NOTE: This is a work of fiction. Names, characters, places, and incidents either are the product of the author's imagination or are used fictitiously. Any resemblance to actual persons, living or dead, business establishments, events, or locales is entirely coincidental.

Published by Oliver-Heber Books

0 9 8 7 6 5 4 3 2 1

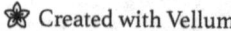 Created with Vellum

1

THE RITZ, PARIS

"More wine?" Mark Redmond asked, hand around the neck of a bottle of *Châteauneuf-du-Pape*. Beneath his stylish and very expensive suit, he was at heart a barbarian, but even he knew it was an excellent wine.

He watched as Harper Kendall, the most enticing woman he'd ever met, pondered his question.

He could almost see the wheels turning in her beautiful head. It really was a good wine and she'd only had one glass to his three. But—was he trying to get her drunk? Trying to seduce her?

No. And yes.

God yes, he was trying to seduce her. He'd been thinking about getting her into his bed since he'd first set eyes on her on the business-class trip from Boston to Paris.

His company had two corporate jets but he had two teams he was sending into failed states and harm's way. He wanted them to get there rested and refreshed, so he had them use the Falcon 8X and the Gulfstream G3.

Going to Paris for a few days before his meeting with the head of a big bank had been a last-minute decision; he hadn't had time off since forever. First class had been fully booked and he'd been amused when he'd caught himself thinking that he'd have to 'settle' for business class. Especially considering how, in his military days, he'd crisscrossed the world in noisy, cold C-130s strapped to the bulkhead, pissing in a bottle.

In the end, going business class was the best thing to happen to him in a long, long time, when he'd seen the beauty sitting in the seat next to his.

"Sure," she said and nudged her glass closer to him. Mark filled the big balloon glass one third full, the canonical amount. Any less and it would have seemed stingy. Any more and she would have reason to suspect he was trying to get her drunk.

He didn't want her drunk, but he did want her happy.

Being with a woman like Harper was challenging, full of hidden pitfalls. Good thing he was a man who relished challenges.

She sipped, watched him a bit warily over the rim of her crystal goblet. "So, do you know Paris well?"

"Been here a few times but always briefly, for work. In and out."

Her lips curled in a smile. "Plumbing supply imports."

"That's right." Mark leaned back and watched her. He always chose the most boring jobs possible for cover. Plumbing supply importer, accountant, tax software salesman. "Fly in, make a deal, fly out. This time I wanted to take a day or two to sightsee. Do you know Paris well?"

"Yes, I do." She took another sip. "I studied French here for a summer, just out of high school, then came for a semester during my master's. I love this city."

There. An opening. Mark waited for her to offer to show him around Paris. But...crickets. He stifled a sigh. Still, he was a man who knew how to make his own opportunities.

"Maybe some other evening you'd have dinner with me. After work. You're here for research, right?"

"Mmm." She smiled. "Some business and some research."

"For that book?" His gorgeous princess had written and published one book and was writing her second, which he really admired. Mark couldn't write a book to save his life. He could kill a man at a thousand yards, but he couldn't write a book.

The smile grew. "That's right. Linking historical political movements to architectural styles. I'm keeping it accessible though, not a cultural tract. Are you interested in architecture, Mark?"

He sat back. "I can't say I'm particularly knowledgeable about architecture and its history. I'll happily read your first book, though. It sounds really interesting."

"Well, that's kind. You don't have to do that."

"I want to." And he did.

"I'll write down the title for you."

He deliberately didn't smile. "The title has three words in it. I think can remember them. So—how about dinner tomorrow evening?"

She didn't answer, just looked at him. Mark understood exactly what was happening. She was consulting her internal self on whether she wanted a second date and the only intel she had on him was what he was giving her. He couldn't tell her who he really was, but he could give her his essence.

He was a good guy. He wasn't going to hurt her. He wanted sex with her badly, more than any woman he could ever remember, but it had to be mutual and he'd treat her well.

He couldn't say that in words but he could show her via his body language. So he sat very, very still, and watched her face. He was probably emitting pheromones by the ton because she was just so goddamn luscious, and he'd had a semi hard-on all through dinner, but that was okay. She had to know he desired her. They'd been in constant contact since they'd first boarded that flight and though he'd been respectful, he'd also made it clear that he was attracted.

Putting it mildly.

She was, too. This was a strong-minded woman and she wouldn't be sitting here having dinner with him at the Ritz if she didn't want to be.

She sighed. "Dinner tomorrow evening? I don't know when I'll finish up with my work."

"Doesn't make any difference," he answered. "I don't have a timetable. I came in early to rest and to sightsee a little." He shrugged. "I've been working really hard lately, and I decided to just relax for a day or two. So I can work around your schedule, no problem."

Harper made a little humming sound, as if thinking over reasons to say no. But she really wanted to say yes. She was a real beauty, so she'd probably spent half her life saying no to men, decisively. She wouldn't be humming if it was a decisive "no".

She looked at their table, at the remains of an excellent meal, at the elegant room. Everyone dressed up, the waiters the most elegant of all, low voices, the gleaming crystal glasses, the chandeliers like crystal clouds, everyone smiling in their comfortable upholstered settees.

It was a feast for all the senses.

"Okay, but not at the Ritz. And it's on me next time."

"Not a chance, but nice try," Mark said. "And we can go anywhere you want. I'm not fussy."

He wasn't. He'd once lived for three weeks on MREs—gummy tubes of nutrients that tasted like cardboard, no matter what the label said. He hadn't liked it but he'd done it.

"We'll see then. Do you want to enter my cell number in your cell?"

"No need." He rattled off her ten-digit number. "You gave me your card on the plane, remember?"

She blinked. "Wow. You have quite a memory if you remember it from my business card."

He shrugged. "I'm good with numbers. My business is figures on spreadsheets. A little less interesting than your business."

She smiled. "I love what I do. So, what do you know about architecture?"

"Not much." He knew nothing about architecture, but he did know a lot about buildings. Particularly how to blow them up. "But I'd love to learn."

She looked around. "This building, for example. The façade dates back to the early eighteenth century and it's part of the seamless Place Vendôme. It's said that this hotel was the first in the world to offer en-suite bathrooms."

He shook his head. "About the only thing I know about its history is that Hemingway 'liberated' the Ritz bar in 1944, gulping down its best wine that they'd hidden from the Nazis, while snipers were still shooting on the outskirts of Paris."

Harper put back her head and laughed, and all Mark could do was stare at her.

In the fanciest restaurant in Paris, possibly in the world, Harper Kendall was the classiest, most beautiful woman there. He watched as she tipped her head back slightly, exposing that long, slim neck, and gave a genuine laugh. It wasn't meant to entice him, she was genuinely amused. But God, she enticed him.

Tilting her head made that shiny mass cascade over her shoulders. Those light gray cat's eyes narrowed as she laughed and she simply took his breathe away.

Though Mark was used to hiding his feelings, something of what was going on inside of him—maybe a sudden surge of testosterone—made her still and look at him, startled and then wary.

One of the many waiters started walking toward them with

the dessert menu in his hand. Mark caught his eye and made a subtle gesture with his hand.

Not now.

You didn't get to be a waiter at the Ritz by being a fool. A simple nod of the head and the waiter faded away.

Mark had other plans for dessert.

He leaned forward slowly. "I know it sounds pedestrian, but I'd really like a Crêpe Suzette for dessert. How about you?"

He kept his voice even, trying to keep himself under control.

"Crêpes Suzette wasn't on the dessert menu. There was pineapple ravioli with wasabi yogurt sauce and Bresse cheese with red onion marmalade." She smiled at him. "I have a good memory too, just not for numbers."

"No, I meant Crêpes Suzette somewhere else. My room, here at the Ritz." Mark covered her slender hand with his. She was acting cool, but her hand was trembling slightly. "It's on the room service menu. And we could pair it with some more champagne or some Grand Marnier."

She looked at him, her luscious mouth slightly open. Silvery-gray eyes wary.

He waited.

She wasn't saying no.

She wasn't saying yes, either.

He kept his hand over hers. It was warm and soft, fingers long and elegant.

Mark's voice was low, without urgency, though desire prickled through his veins. "I have a suite. We could sit and talk in private." He looked around the beautiful room, full of customers. "Where no one could bother us."

He tightened his hold on her hand, but just slightly. He had big strong hands and he didn't want to hurt her or make her feel coerced. She watched him silently, hand still slightly trembling under his.

"I promise you that nothing will happen that you don't want to happen. If all you want is a Crêpe Suzette and a glass of champagne or Grand Marnier and a chat, that's fine. I'll take it and I'll be happy. But I won't hide from you that I'd like more."

She still didn't say anything. Just sat there, eyes looking into his, darting back and forth, making little silver flashes like lightning.

"Your call." Then Mark shut up.

Maybe more words would convince her. She was a writer, eloquent words probably mattered to her. But he didn't have eloquence in him. He was a straightforward kind of guy. He'd said what he needed to say. He'd told her he wanted her. If he elaborated on that, said that he was burning up with desire, that he wanted her like he wanted his next breath, he might scare her away.

Also, he'd made it clear that she could trust him. And she could, even if it killed him.

He waited to see what she would say. He couldn't remember wanting anything more than he wanted her. Like the song said, every move she made fascinated him. His entire body was tense, waiting for her response. He was tense between his legs, too. He had to will the hard-on down by thinking of Afghanistan, thinking of the men who died or were maimed there.

It was hard though. Afghanistan was now seven thousand miles and years away but Harper was right here, right now. She was a stunner with light brown hair that turned silver in the light, matching her silvery-gray eyes with a dark blue rim. They nearly glowed in the dark. She had a heart-shaped face with silky-smooth pale skin and a mouth that was made for kissing. All this paired with small, perfect breasts, a tiny waist and long legs.

But more than that she was smart, with a dry sense of humor and a bottomless fund of knowledge of the world. He'd never met anyone quite like her, and he wanted her so much it made his hands itch and his dick twitch.

He wanted to make love to her, but it had to be mutual. She had to want it too. He'd rather tear out his own throat than hurt her or force her.

She still didn't say anything, but he could see her rolling the idea around in that beautiful head of hers. That was okay. He was a patient man. He could wait. And for her? For her, he'd wait a long, long time.

Now that she was in his head, he couldn't even imagine desiring someone else. She was everything he could possibly want in a woman. Smart, classy, gorgeous.

She waited for a beat. Two.

Then she twisted her hand under his.

For a horrific moment, Mark thought she was going to pull her hand away, get up and walk out.

But no.

Her palm came to rest against his palm and her fingers clasped his.

His heart gave a sharp thump in his chest.

It was a yes.

2

Yes.

Harper Kendall sighed.

It looked like she was going to say yes to this guy she'd met on a plane not twenty-four hours ago.

She'd splurged on a business-class ticket hoping that a middle-of-the-week flight might actually allow her to travel alone. But along had come this guy in the pod right next to hers, looking sharply at her, and she'd sighed to herself. Not only had she spent all that money to not travel alone but she'd have to fend off some guy.

But it turned out he had perfect manners, had helped her with her luggage both on departure and arrival, and had insisted on giving her a lift into town with his car and driver.

Harper wasn't born yesterday and the offer of a lift...well. But it turned out that there was a taxi strike, his driver looked legitimate and normal, and Mark Redmond looked legitimate and normal, and she'd accepted.

It had been like having some tall, good-looking butler. He'd taken care of the luggage, asked the name of her hotel and had her taken directly there.

Then at the very last moment, he'd asked her out to dinner. At the Ritz. To her surprise, she'd accepted. And now he was asking her up to his room. And to her surprise, she was thinking of accepting. Actually *had* accepted.

That was *so* not her. Harper was amazingly picky, always had been. So picky she hadn't had a partner in, what? Two years? And she was going to break her dry spell with a man she didn't know at all.

Well, she knew he had an amazingly boring job. Plumbing supplies importer. He hadn't even tried to impress her with his job like most men did. Though he was clearly doing well with plumbing supplies if he could afford business class to Paris, a private car meeting him at the airport and a room at the Ritz. Most men making that kind of money would have bragged about it, at least a little. But Mark hadn't, not at all.

He wasn't much of a talker, either. Though what he did say was smart.

He gave a gentle smile and rose, lifting her up by the hand. Another couple of points in his favor. He did not give a smug male smile, the smile of the guy who'd scored a hot one and was really pleased with himself. No, he wasn't giving those vibes off at all. He was calm and pleasant. So much so that Harper was absolutely positive that if she said no at the last minute, he'd be okay with it and not go ballistic.

She wouldn't do it, she wasn't a tease. But still, it was nice to know that if she did get cold feet at the last minute, there wouldn't be a tussle.

Some instinct told her that there would never be a tussle with Mark Redmond, which was a *huge* plus in his favor.

A year ago, she'd met someone at a fundraiser for her museum and he'd been superficially charming. They had friends in common and he had a great job in Washington, DC, which he'd repeatedly told her. Over and over, actually. It didn't take long to realize that he was a real jerk. The unredeemable kind. The kind whose *molecules* were jerks. He'd cornered her outside, pushed her against the wall and kissed her, hard. Hard enough to hurt.

She'd pushed at his shoulders, run out into the street, hailed a taxi and watched him gesticulate angrily in the middle of the street as the taxi pulled away. His handsome face had become ugly as he'd spewed obscenities she couldn't hear.

That wouldn't happen with Mark. Liam had given off bad vibes almost immediately. Mark hadn't once made her uneasy.

They walked out of the restaurant together. *Les Jardins de L'Espadon*. One of the most famous restaurants in the world and she'd wanted to eat here since her first trip to Paris when she was eighteen.

The food had been fabulous. But, of course. The Ritz.

The whole experience was exquisite. They were walking on the most magnificent pink and cream carpet she'd ever seen. Heading for the exit, they passed the huge circular console that marked the center of the room. On it was an enormous Chinese vase—Ming, unless she was mistaken—with a floral arrangement as big as Mark, the flowers of the season cascading from it. Calla lilies, tulips, camellias, hyacinths, irises, tightly packed white roses. The smell was heady as they walked past.

He'd taken her hand and was guiding her out, not too fast and not too slow, looking ahead of them but seeming to have 360° awareness of the space around them. There was a knot of people waiting for the second sitting and Harper braced herself, but he guided them through the small crowd like a dream. She wasn't jostled, she wasn't even touched.

She'd noticed that before, when they'd stood up on landing after the long flight. Usually she was jostled and bumped around and often some clueless passenger would step on her feet. Instead, Mark had quietly reached up to grab her wheelie and raincoat and somehow formed a barrier around her as they'd shuffled out of business class onto the jetway.

Being with Mark was like being in a bubble of protection.

He guided them across the elaborate lobby and before she knew it they were in the elevator. She caught glimpses of herself in the brass columns framing the wooden panels. She looked pale and worried.

What was she doing?

Without glancing at her, Mark brought the back of her hand to his mouth. His hand was so warm, as was his mouth. It was like he breathed heat into her.

"I said Crêpes Suzette because I like them, but we can have anything you want. The room service menu includes raspberry cheesecake and crème brûlée." He turned his head and smiled down at her. His face was sharply chiseled with high cheekbones and lean cheeks. His default expression was sober. Almost grim, actually, as if his boring business were a dangerous profession. His rare smiles changed the contours of his face. He didn't smile that often but when he did, the smile reached his dark eyes. "Your choice. Your choice in everything."

Standing so close to him, she was overwhelmingly aware of how tall and amazingly well built he was. Certainly for a plumbing supplies importer. She'd have thought that an importer would be the kind of businessman who sat at the computer all day comparing spreadsheets. But Mark had huge shoulders tapering down to a lean waist and carried himself with athletic grace.

He was much larger than she was, but she didn't feel overwhelmed by him. He was standing close to her but not so close she felt smothered. Their shoulders touched and of course they were holding hands. It felt ...good.

She looked up at him. "I love Crêpes Suzette. There was a crêperie on my street when I lived here as a student. The shop had a little stand out on the sidewalk where they'd prepare fresh crêpes for you at a third of the price. I used to love buckwheat crêpes with Nutella."

"Hmm." Mark furrowed his brow. "I could try ordering those. I'm sure the chef knows how."

Harper laughed, relaxing a little. He looked perplexed, as if someone had just commanded him to play Mozart but he didn't play the piano.

"Don't worry about it. I love it when they light the Grand Marnier."

"Me, too." He smiled at her. "I like it when you laugh. You don't laugh often."

There really wasn't an answer to that. Luckily, the elevator pinged and the doors opened onto a hallway with a light turquoise runner with huge roses on it and consoles with vases of flowers in front of elaborately beveled mirrors. The vaulted ceiling was frescoed with roses. The air was scented with lavender.

It could have passed for any ancient castle in any fairy tale. She'd seen the first *Beauty and the Beast* a thousand times. She was surprised there weren't human hands holding light sconces along the walls.

Mark turned right, still holding her hand. Harper was looking around with interest when they stopped in front of a door. He didn't seem to have a card key in his hand but suddenly he was holding the door open for her.

She walked in and nearly gasped. The suite was gorgeous. They were in a small sitting room with a light green brocade couch and two matching armchairs. It smelled of a rose-based potpourri. Mark switched on two table lamps with crystal bases and cream silk shades. He took off his jacket and held his hand out for hers, tossing both of them onto an armchair.

She heard him speaking softly into the phone while she walked around, touching the armchairs, the pearl-inlaid picture frames, an ormolu clock on a side table.

The door to the bedroom was closed. She still hadn't completely decided about that part of the evening. But right now, she was enjoying being in this beautiful room with this man.

"It's a real suite," she said. "At the Ritz. I imagined my being here one day but only when I'm 50 and have made my money. The plumbing supply importing business must be going great guns."

"I have a very generous boss. Me. And he gives me a very generous expense account," he replied. He sat on the couch, making a huge dent in the cushions. He patted the area next to him. Okay. She didn't have any problem sitting next to him. It felt good, feeling his body heat, brushing his powerful shoulder with her own.

Harper shook her head. "I like your boss. He pays for a car to pick you up at the airport and for a suite at the Ritz. My boss is so cheap he won't pay for a taxi from the airport even when I arrive late in an unknown city, let alone a car and a driver."

Mark frowned. "It's important to arrive rested when you're going on a business trip. Your boss should understand that. Not to mention safety issues."

Harper gave a light laugh at the thought of Ivan the Terrible caring one way or another what shape she'd be in after a business trip. "My boss is a sociopath and he's incapable of understanding anything of the sort. Though he is very generous with our budget when it comes to himself. No, this trip is my own research trip, paid for with my own money. Which is why I sprang for business class and a nice hotel. Nothing like this, though."

She looked around the room admiringly. Everything was just perfect, she thought. The many floral arrangements were fresh, the marble and wood gleamed, absolutely everything was pleasing.

Including the man sitting beside her.

For the first time, she admitted to herself how attracted she was to him. It had sneaked up on her stealthily. He was *so* not her type, though to be honest, her type had proved disappointing, over and over again.

He was smart but not an intellectual, well dressed without being trendy, knowledgeable about how the world worked without being a bore.

Since he wasn't her type at all, the attraction had been slow to burn, without her even noticing it.

Maybe she was attracted because he was just so *male,* without being a creep in any way. He just gave off these amazing male vibes in the old-fashioned sense of male. He was an adult; most of the men she dated felt like kids in comparison, fretting about status and money and needing for her to be impressed.

Mark did none of those things. What he did do was throw a veil of protection around her, which was crazy. Harper didn't need protecting, she could make her own way in the world just fine. Nonetheless, over the course of that long flight, he'd managed to make pleasant, non-boring conversation while reassuring her with his body language alone. She was a nervous flier and when they'd hit a bad patch of turbulence midway across the Atlantic, she'd clutched his arm instinctively. He'd put his hand over hers and had given her an amusing rundown of the movie they'd both been watching.

He'd taken her mind off the turbulence, he'd made her laugh and she'd completely let go of her fear.

Mark Redmond was big and tall and strong, and though she thought herself completely unsusceptible to those things, her hormones had sandbagged her. Who knew she had hormones that could take over and drive?

"Your boss is a moron," he said, completely seriously.

It startled a laugh out of her because it was so true.

"There," Mark said, running the back of a long finger down her face. "There's that laugh again. I like it when you laugh."

She heard the words, but it was as if they were coming from

very far away. They jumbled in her head, meaningless. What did penetrate was the heat his soft touch sparked under her skin, as if his fingers shot electricity. Close up, his size was almost overwhelming. He'd taken his jacket off and his shoulders and biceps strained the elegant white shirt. His thighs, too, were huge.

A shiver of sexual excitement ran through her body, so alien she almost didn't recognize it.

But he did.

Somehow, he latched on to what was happening with her faster than she did. Every part of her was open to him, something unfurling inside her like another person waking up, looking around and liking what she saw.

Her eyes were open wide, as were her nostrils and mouth, as if she had to take in more oxygen to deal with her body's excitement. Her chest expanded, breasts swelling against her bra. She didn't dare look down at her chest because she could feel her nipples growing harder, something completely out of her control.

Please don't look down, she silently begged Mark. And—thank you, God!—he didn't. His eyes were fixed on hers.

And below the waist... Mmm. Her sex somehow opened and softened, as if she were being touched by him.

The air between them almost shimmered with sexual tension. She'd never felt anything like this before.

Without thinking about it, she moved forward because there were magnetic lines between them and that's how it had to be. She had to be in his arms, right now.

Though his expression was always bland, gentle, now he looked hard. The muscles of his face were pulled tight, nostrils white, brackets around his mouth. He looked under strain, but it wasn't that. This was male arousal, and though she'd never seen arousal quite as intense as this before, she instinctively recognized it. It was something beyond experience and beyond words—an instinct as old as mankind.

They moved toward each other, her mouth slowly opening, eyes slowly closing...

A soft knock sounded at the door.

Her eyes opened, she took in a deep breath and pulled away. Like a swimmer about ready to take the high dive then stepping back at the last minute.

It was as if something broke.

Mark sat up straight and that hard look disappeared. His mouth turned up at one corner.

"The crêpes," he said, and sighed.

"What?"

Harper couldn't follow what he was saying.

"The Crêpes Suzette." Mark dropped a quick kiss on her mouth, their first. So fast she didn't have time to react. He walked quickly to the door and opened it. A tuxedoed waiter stood in the hallway pushing a restaurant cart.

Oh. *Of course!* How stupid of her. They'd ordered Crêpes Suzette and she'd completely forgotten about it. Her hormones had wiped about 50 IQ points from her mind.

This was not good. Whatever was going to happen between her and Mark, she needed to keep her wits about her. It was never good to let one's guard down. She believed that fervently.

And here he'd reduced her brain to cream of wheat with no effort at all.

The waiter rolled in the cart, stopped it and removed a huge silver cover. Underneath were two rose-patterned dessert plates, a long-handled copper saucepan, a bottle of Grand Marnier and a bottle of champagne in an ice bucket. He pulled a table away from the wall, set two chairs, and placed the dessert plates with orange-infused, folded crêpes and two crystal flutes on the table, and the ice bucket on a stand.

The waiter tipped some Grand Marnier into the saucepan,

lit it, and poured the flaming alcohol over the crêpes. Mark accompanied him to the door, discreetly handing him a tip. By the time he returned, the flames had gone out and the crêpes looked luscious and rich, glistening with orange marmalade and the liqueur.

She smiled up at him. "You missed the best part."

He held out her chair. "No, the best part is the eating."

"So true."

He popped the cork of the champagne and filled their glasses. He lifted his and gently pinged her glass. The lovely tone of fine crystal filled the air. "Here's to you."

Harper sipped, on more even ground now. For a second, her hormones had got the better of her. This was familiar, though maybe unusually pleasing in all ways. Beautiful hotel room, excellent champagne, superb crêpes.

And the man himself...wow. He just seemed to get better and better. Not at all the boring businessman seatmate she thought had been her fate when she'd settled in the plane. She'd been prepared to be bored and maybe even annoyed all the way across the Atlantic.

Instead...here she was, with a man who hadn't said anything foolish or self-serving yet and who exuded a quiet but potent male appeal. And was really built.

Was that it? Was she that shallow? Was she so intensely attracted to a man because of his muscles?

She tipped her glass to his again, for the pleasure of hearing that pure silvery note of crystal ring out. "To you, too."

He smiled at her over his glass, put it down and cut his first slice of the Crêpes Suzette. "Mm." He closed his eyes, opened them again and looked straight into hers. "Delicious."

Her heart gave a huge thump in her chest.

Oh, dear.

"Try it." Mark cut a bite of his own crêpe and held it out to her. "It's fabulous."

She closed her eyes as she chewed. Damn, it *was* fabulous. She opened them to find him staring at her, heat in his dark eyes. They glowed as if lit from inside his head. He wanted her, it was plain to see.

"God," he said. "You're sexy when you eat. But then you're sexy when you're not eating, too."

She chewed and swallowed until her plate was empty, then put her fork down on her plate. "I don't know how to respond to that."

His hand covered hers again, huge, hot and calloused, unusually so for a businessman. "You're right. It was a dumb thing to say. My only excuse is that it's true. I want you."

There, it was out in the open.

Harper had a perverse mechanism in her. She often took a step back when the man took a step forward.

That mechanism was broken.

Everything felt wound up inside her. She couldn't go forward and she couldn't go backward. She didn't know what to do.

But Mark did. He curled his hand around hers, leaned forward and kissed her.

And that awful grinding feeling of everything inside her coming to a jagged halt ended. Inside, she melted, everything becoming honey smooth.

He only touched her with his mouth, but it was enough to infuse warmth in her down to her toes. He lifted his mouth, kissed her again from a different, deeper angle. His hands rose to slide through her hair, cup her head. Oh, God. The kiss became deeper and deeper, hot and so enticing her heart started pounding in her chest.

They rose together, as one, took a step forward, as one. Mark was kissing her so deeply she couldn't breathe and had to breathe through him. She needed this kiss more than she needed oxygen. Who needed oxygen? Oxygen was everywhere. This kiss...this kiss was really rare.

It was as if she'd never been kissed before, the feeling almost electric when her tongue met his. She reached up, trying to embrace those broad shoulders, loving the feel of steely muscle against her arms. Mark kept one hand cupping the back of her head, the other on her back, pressing her against him.

He was all unyielding muscle, more like steel or wood than human flesh. Something else was like steel or wood, too. His erect penis was huge and hard against her belly. She gasped when she felt it and his kiss deepened, lips and teeth nibbling against her mouth, tongue stroking hers deep inside.

Harper curled her fingers into his shoulders, but there was no purchase. Beneath the fine cotton of his shirt was muscle so hard she couldn't dent it with her fingertips to gain purchase. But something in her wanted him closer to her, wanted to explore this new world of heat flaring inside her.

She stepped even closer to him and rubbed her belly against his penis.

Oh God, it swelled even bigger, like a powerful animal flexing against her belly. A vision of that huge penis entering her flared in her mind and her vagina clenched, trying to hold him inside her, even though they weren't having sex.

Yet.

So that solved that issue. Would she or wouldn't she? Definitely *yes*, she would. This amazing excitement, this electric heat inside her was new territory that simply had to be discovered. Nothing like this had ever happened to her before in her twenty-eight years. For all she knew, another twenty-eight years might go by before it happened again.

He kissed her neck while undressing her, distracting her so much she was almost naked before she realized what he was doing.

It was probably a good idea he was undressing her because her hands felt magnetically attached to his shoulders. She let go of him only to lift her arms so he could slip off her silk top.

"Beautiful outfit," he murmured against the skin of her neck. "But you look even better out of it." He stepped back slightly and she missed the warmth of his body so close to hers. That span of cold air seemed absolutely intolerable.

It seemed intolerable for him, too, because he undressed with the speed of light, tossing his clothes over the back of the sofa. His pants slid off to rustle to the carpet, lying there like the shed skin of a mysterious jungle animal, the fine dark wool crumpled on the floor.

She glanced down, then back up at him. "Your pants are going to crease."

They stared at each other.

What had just come out of her mouth? She drew in a deep breath, absolutely mortified.

"I'm so sorry," she gasped. "I can't believe I said that."

Here she was, minutes away from what she was sure would be the best sex of her life, and she was talking about possible *creases* in his *pants?* How uncool was that? What was wrong with her?

There was a dent in his cheek that might be a smile. He ran the back of his forefinger down the side of her face. "You're nervous."

Ordinarily Harper would never admit that. Why should she be nervous? It was just sex. But...she was.

"No," she said. "Maybe."

Mark bent his head to her. "I don't want you nervous." He kissed the side of her mouth, moved his lips over her jawline, down the side of her neck. He licked a spot then nipped it. Not a bite, not quite. He scraped his teeth down the tendon in her neck and she broke out in goose bumps. "I want you relaxed. Pleasured."

His voice had turned so deep it reverberated in her diaphragm. Oh, God. She'd turned into a human tuning fork, especially attuned to him.

"We're getting there," she gasped.

Mark didn't answer. His mouth moved to her ear, licking inside it, and a deep shudder ran through her body and goose bumps broke out over her forearms. She'd never really realized that the ear was such an erogenous zone.

Everything was an erogenous zone. Her ear, her neck, under her chin, wherever his mouth wandered. When it wandered lower, licking and pulling at her nipple, the pleasure was almost too much. She was shuddering, rubbing herself against his groin, her vagina clenching even though it was still empty.

Heat filled her, from her lungs out. A blistering heat as if the sun had suddenly come up inside her, heat and energy crackling through her, down to her fingertips and toes.

Mark kissed his way up her chest to her mouth and then they were kissing wildly, trying to get as much skin-to-skin contact as possible. He was holding her tightly, almost hurting her but not quite, and she scrambled to press herself against him, against that long, strong, hot body.

She had contact, but somehow it wasn't enough. She moved in his arms, rubbing against him like a cat. She *felt* like a cat. If she could, she'd purr and she definitely wanted to lick him, just lap him up. Everything felt so damned *good*. Every part of her, from her hair to her toes.

Mark lifted his mouth just a fraction of an inch from hers, as if too much distance would be unbearable. She knew exactly how he felt.

"Bed?" he gasped.

"God, yes," she answered. An image, a heart-stopping image, filled her head. She was spread-eagled on a bed and Mark was on top of her, slowly moving in and out of her. She saw it as if she were looking down from the ceiling, watching his buttocks move as he made love to her. Their hands were intertwined and his strong thighs held hers apart.

She shivered and her vagina clenched again. He wasn't in her, not yet, but she could feel his hard, hot penis against her belly and it didn't take much to imagine them already having sex.

Mark tilted slightly, then the world tilted and she realized he was carrying her toward the bedroom. It was amazing. He showed no stress, not even his breathing changed. They were still kissing, her arms tight around his strong neck. Incredibly, he didn't seem to have to look at where they were going, even though the living room area was full of furniture. He didn't trip and fall as she surely would have.

It was like a scene in a movie—a sexy movie. Both of them naked, kissing, and she was being carried to bed. They'd have to pixelate his erect penis, though.

They were in his bedroom. He hadn't turned on the lights, there was just faint light from the living room spilling into the bedroom. It didn't reach the bed, which was mysterious and shadowy.

What kind of lover was Mark going to be? Slow and languid, enthusiastic and rough? She didn't like rough sex but something told her she might like Mark's rough sex.

He set her beside the bed for a moment and held her by the waist as he pulled down the flowered duvet. He was a broad shadow in the darkness of the big room, discernable more by the heat he was giving off than by sight.

Throwing back the duvet gave off a cloud of lavender scent, offset by his smell, pleasingly male. She'd barely had time to breathe in the smells when he picked her up again, effortlessly, and placed her in the center of the bed. A moment later, his heavy weight settled on her.

His hands cupped her head and his hard thighs opened

hers. She was completely at his mercy but she didn't feel constrained in any way. Though he surrounded her, was weighing her down, was holding her legs open with his, she knew he wasn't overpowering her.

Mark dropped his head until his forehead touched hers. "Are you okay?" he asked. It was dark but she could see a furrow between his black eyebrows.

Was she *okay*?

"Any better and I'd be dead," she gasped. He barked out a laugh, as if against his will, and she was charmed by the sound.

He kissed her, lifted his head. "You're so perfect," he said, completely seriously.

Whoa. Not all of her lovers thought so. As a matter of fact, a lot of her lovers had been disappointed. Too cold, they said. Too unresponsive. She didn't feel cold and unresponsive now, though.

"Wait until we're finished and then we'll see." Something in her voice, an unintended bitterness, made him widen his eyes in surprise.

"Some guy thought you *weren't* perfect?" Mark's voice held astonishment, as if the thought were completely alien to him.

Now was not the time to have the ghosts of other men in the bed with them. Not when she had questions of her own. Harper made a noncommittal sound as she ran her hands over his broad, strong back. His broad, strong, *scarred* back. She could feel small scars, big scars with keloid scar tissue and, on his upper back, a round, puckered scar that was echoed on his chest.

"What are these?" she asked.

"You mean you don't think *I'm* perfect?"

She gave a half-hearted slap to his shoulder. "You know what I mean. What are all these scars? Have you been to war?"

"Not to war," he said. "To dojos."

"Dojos?"

Mark nodded. "A dojo is a martial arts gym that—"

"I know what a dojo is. A friend of mine goes to a dojo for tai chi but she isn't covered in scars."

Mark kissed her neck, exactly that point that made her mindless. She tipped her head to give him better access and closed her eyes. Mark stretched out even more on top of her, so that every inch of her front met every inch of his front, his huge, erect penis like a hot steel tube along her belly.

He bit her, very lightly, right...*there*, and she jolted with pleasure, breaking out in goose bumps.

"You like that," he murmured. His deep voice held pleasure not smugness. He enjoyed pleasuring her.

"Mmmm." He bit her very lightly again then licked the spot. Her hips rose, rubbing against his, his penis so incredibly hot. An involuntary groan of pleasure escaped him.

"I think I seem to remember you like this, too." And he licked her nipple.

Harper gave a huge, whole-body shudder.

But they'd been talking about something...

"What are those scars about?" she gasped, just before he suckled her breast. Like a child would, only this wasn't a child. She looked down at that dark head, strong hand tenderly cupping her breast, his shoulders so broad they overwhelmed her, cutting off her view of everything but him.

"Mark?"

"Yeah?" He lifted his head and looked at her breast, the nipple deep pink and wet. He blew on the nipple and she shook.

They were minutes away from full-blown sex but before he entered her body, she wanted answers.

"Scars," she gasped.

He answered her without lifting his gaze from her breasts. "I've been going to dojos since I was a boy. They weren't fun places serving expensive water with lemon slices where you went to keep fit. They were dojos where you trained seriously in martial arts and where people got hurt. For example, that round scar you felt?"

He lifted his head and pinned her with his dark gaze. She nodded.

"That was a bo staff — a training stick. Went right through me. The scars just show that I took my martial arts seriously."

Did he ever. The scars, those muscles—the man was seriously strong and built. But he didn't look like a gym rat; he looked like a man who used his body well.

He smiled down at her, looking dangerously hot. Heavy-lidded dark eyes, skin tight, mouth slightly swollen. Insanely attractive, not a bland businessman at all. "We done talking?" he asked, and she nodded.

Yeah. She was done talking. Her body was on fire for him and she needed him inside her. Right. Now.

Harper arched against him, rubbing against his belly, the tip of his penis slightly wet, nature's way of easing men inside women.

He didn't need it, though. She could feel herself, soft and wet, very ready for him.

"Now, Mark," she whispered.

"God, yeah."

Mark reached out a long arm to the gray travel kit on the bedside console and took out a foil package. In a moment, he was ready, shifting himself so that they were nose to nose, his hips directly above hers, ready to enter her.

She could feel him, hot and stiff, at her entrance. He placed both hands on the bed on either side of her head and lifted himself, big biceps flexing. He was poised; hard, muscled torso hovering above her. He glanced down their bodies and she followed his gaze.

It was the most erotic sight she'd ever seen. She was fully open to him, legs spread, his penis just at her entrance. She was much paler than him, their two skin tones making such a sexy contrast. She looked almost vulnerable against the hard planes of his heavily-muscled body but she didn't feel vulnerable. He could crush her in a second. She was beneath him, open to him but not vulnerable to him. There was a strong current of energy between them, almost visible shifts of power and a lot of the power was hers.

She felt strong and vital and about ready to die if he didn't *move.*

Harper clasped his buttocks and pressed down and he entered her. Slowly. It cost him a great deal to move so slowly. His jaws were clenched, eyes narrowed, biceps bulging. A bead of sweat ran down his face, off his chin, onto her breast.

Harper caught it with a finger, putting the finger in her mouth. His sweat tasted salty, sexy.

Mark gave out a huff of breath, as if he were lifting weights, but he didn't slam into her. He entered by slow degrees and she was glad he did. He was huge. Moving so slowly, there wasn't any pain but at times a little discomfort. She opened her legs more as he slowly entered her.

"God!" Another drop of sweat fell on her. "You're so tight."

Harper shrugged, curling her fingers around his steely shoulders. "It's been a while."

Mark closed his eyes as if in pain and lowered himself slowly until his entire weight was on her. It felt good, like he was making love to her whole body. He cupped her head in his big hands and entered her, moving faster now. It should have hurt but it didn't because she was so ready for him. She was entirely open to him. Sex, arms, legs, mouth, heart...

Then Mark was inside her, completely in. He lifted his head, taking her lower lip in his mouth, biting it lightly. "Have to move now," he said, deep voice low and hoarse.

As an answer. Harper opened even further to him, lifting

her hips until he was embedded in her to the root. She felt entirely taken by him, her body completely his.

Mark moved his hands down to clasp her hips and started moving, gently at first, then harder. The beautiful inlaid head-board began beating a tattoo against the wall as he rocked harder and harder inside her. The friction was incredible, she was burning up, an enormous ball of heat building inside her until, with a cry she fell into the abyss, heart pounding, legs and arms holding him as if she would never let go.

He followed immediately with a shout, swelling inside her, shaking then exploding.

They clutched each other tightly and then, with a huge sigh, Mark relaxed, placing his head on the pillow next to hers. She turned her head and their noses touched. She smiled at him and he smiled back, tucking a lock of her hair behind her ear.

"Wow," he said. "Just...wow."

3

Hours later, she fell asleep like a rock. Well, he used her hard toward the end. That first time had been merely a taste, the result of being in a state of semi-arousal since the day before, when he'd seen her for the first time. So the first time had been fast, getting something out of his system. Then he'd gotten down to business, making love to her so intensely at times he thought he'd pass out.

He was curled around her, like two spoons, her head pillowed on his arm. Mark tightened his arms slightly, delighted with the feel of her. The long, slim limbs, that amazingly kissable neck, the two perfect dimples on the top of her ass. God, such soft skin. He wanted to touch her all over, as he'd done during the night, but he knew he shouldn't. Shit. She was sleeping, probably jet-lagged.

He was jet-lagged, too, but he couldn't sleep. God, no. Way too revved. Maybe part of it was that he hadn't had sex in... what? Who knew? A long time, anyway. He actually couldn't remember the name of the last woman he'd had sex with. Her face was a little fuzzy, too.

Well, he'd had back-to-back missions for well over a year

now, not to mention being owner of a company that was growing insanely fast.

Rule number one on a mission was focus. Rule number two —no sex. To be truthful, he hadn't missed it, hadn't noticed its absence, busy building his company into one of the finest security companies in the world.

But that no-sex rule had changed overnight. The night with Harper had been overwhelming, like feasting on wonderful food after a year of fasting. But the thing was, it was more Harper herself than the sex.

She was beautiful and mysterious and as self-contained as a cat. Yet in bed she was pure flame.

He'd grown fully erect against her bottom, starting to pull away from her. No use being a hound dog. To his surprise, she wiggled that delectable bottom against his hard-on and he abandoned his not-being-a-hound-dog-and-let-Harper-sleep policy immediately.

He *was* a hound dog where she was concerned. And if she was rubbing against him, she was up for more.

Yeah. Good. So was he.

He put his face against her neck, sniffing like a dog. She smelled so damned good. "Good morning," he whispered directly into her ear.

"Morning." Her voice had a little early morning hoarseness to it. Throaty, sexy.

He kissed her neck, licked behind her ear. She shivered a little. "How are we feeling this morning, hmm?"

Harper gave a breathy laugh. "I don't know how *we're* feeling, but I'm feeling pretty good."

"Me, too." He was feeling more than pretty good. His erection was so hard it was as if he hadn't had sex for years, instead of spending half the night inside her.

He had *some* control, but not much. He could do a little foreplay if he had to. Foreplay with Harper was really exciting.

But being inside her was even better and he wanted to be inside her *now*.

Mark lifted up on one elbow so he could look over her shoulder and see her fully. She was just so amazingly beautiful all over. Perfect ivory skin, tiny waist, round hips, long sleek legs...mmm. And those breasts, like vanilla ice cream cones with little cherries on top. Cherries that became deep pink when she was aroused. Right now, her nipples were turning rosy again.

He'd never forget the sight of her coming, belly muscles pulling with each contraction, nipples red and hard, mouth wet and open to pull in air.

Mark had always closed his eyes when coming. He hadn't even realized it until he had sex with Harper and he couldn't close his eyes, not for a second, because he didn't want to miss even a moment of her pleasure.

Her pleasure was amazing.

He buried his face in her neck because he'd figured out that her neck was a real turn-on for her. Lots of places were her turn-ons, but the neck was special. He licked her and scraped his teeth along the tendon and felt her shudder in his arms. Felt her breath speeding up.

Was it having other effects, too?

His hand slid from her throat, over her breasts, over that flat belly, down to her mound. She lifted her leg to give him access and he slid a finger inside and—*yes!*

Soft and wet. Ready.

God.

He whispered in her ear, "Harper." He could feel her shudder.

"Yes," she whispered back.

Yes, an answer to her name, or yes, they could have sex right now?

His body decided for him. He reached for a condom—their

fourth—and smoothed it on, fitting his hips to her backside.

He opened her up with his fingers and slid inside. She was still tight but a night of sex made his entry easier.

Just the thought of it—that Harper's sex was being shaped by his penis—made him swell inside her.

"Wow. I felt that." Harper gave a half laugh. "That must have been one sexy thought."

He was deep inside her now, held tightly. "You have no idea." He started moving slowly, gripping her hips.

She looked over her shoulder at him. "Tell me."

Mark shook his head, moving inside her more quickly.

"Tell me now." And she gave him a sultry smile over her shoulder, completely irresistible. He'd have to be made of stone to resist, and he wasn't made of stone.

"All right," he panted, moving fast. "I was thinking that you're a little less tight." He moved faster, harder. "I was thinking my cock is shaping you, so that at some point, you'll be made just for me, exactly right for me."

Her eyes widened and he felt her explosion, from the inside out. Her sex gripped him hard, clenching and unclenching, her breath leaving her in one long cry. He stayed with her, moving in time with the convulsions until finally he, too, went up in flames, holding her tightly.

He never wanted to let her go. They were a little sticky with sweat and very sticky in the groin area.

They both fell back asleep, Mark waking up when Harper left the bed. There was an early morning glow around the heavy curtains. Checking his watch he saw that it was seven thirty.

Harper disappeared into the bathroom. A moment later, he heard the shower come on. Most women lingered in showers—and the Ritz's shower was amazing. Huge marble cubicle, showerheads everywhere, one of which was lavender-scented. He expected her to take her time, but in a few moments, he heard the shower turn off. She didn't linger over drying, either.

This wasn't good.

His whole plan for the day included the two of them lingering over pleasurable things every second they could. A businesslike shower didn't bode well.

Sure enough, she came out wrapped in a huge soft towel and headed straight for her clothes.

She didn't look him in the eye, intent on getting dressed as quickly as possible.

Was she going to do a bunk on him? Just disappear? Well, that wasn't going to happen.

She was definitely going to try that I'm-too-busy-to-make-plans-with-you thing. He recognized it because he'd pulled that one himself, often.

He sat quietly, watching her not looking at him. In only a few minutes, she was dressed, combed, made up, looking exactly as she had last night. Beautifully groomed and put together, which was no mean feat, considering how they'd spent the night. You couldn't tell she'd spent the night fucking, except for the faint hickey right where her neck met her shoulder. Mark usually paid attention and didn't leave marks on women, but he'd been coming at the time and his control had been shot.

"Well," she began.

"My driver is downstairs," Mark said. "Waiting for you."

She blinked. "I'm going to have to go back to my hotel to change." She looked down at herself, at the elegant evening outfit. Pale blue and slinky. "I have some research to do and I need more casual wear."

"Fine." Mark stood and quickly dressed in jeans, a linen sweater and a windbreaker. Ready for anything. "We'll swing by your hotel and then I'll accompany you where you have to go."

Mark could actually see her mind whirring. It would, yes,

be nice to have a car and a driver at her disposal. Paris was a busy city and hard to get around in. But the car and the driver came with *him*.

Did she want him?

Yes and no. He could read it clearly. She wanted to spend more time with him. But she also wanted to get her business done.

"I won't be in your way," he said quietly. "Promise."

She looked away then back at him. "It's not really that," she said with a sigh. "I have some research to take care of at the Louvre. I've already booked my ticket but it would take you hours to get in. Sometimes people book a week in advance, otherwise you have to spend a couple of hours waiting in line. I'm really sorry, but we need to split up."

Mark kept a deadpan face though inside he was grinning. It was as if the universe were pointing a huge red arrow at Harper. It was a coincidence that no one would possibly believe.

"Well, that's interesting." He lifted his briefcase, opened it and, *yup*. There it was. He'd been annoyed to find the printout of the entry ticket to the Louvre with a Post-it—*A little culture will do you good.*

But right now? Right now, he could kiss his secretary on the mouth, blue lipstick and piercings and all.

He unfolded the printout and showed it to her. Her eyes widened. Just in case she missed it, Mark tapped the date of the ticket. Today. An all-day pass.

"Isn't that a coincidence?" he said cheerfully. "I was planning on going to the Louvre anyway. I won't bother you. I'll just tag along and look at what's on the walls while you do your thing."

He met her annoyed eyes and smiled. "And this evening, I'd love to take you out to dinner."

4

Harper should have been peeved that Mark was tagging along. This trip was crucial to her future and to freeing herself from her nasty boss. The article she was going to write based on her research at the Louvre was due to be published in her museum's newsletter and would be referenced in the inaugural edition of N/DESIGN, a new quarterly design magazine she was co-founding with three young designers. They had advertising lined up and a good distribution platform.

Maybe even in museum shops, including the Louvre shop. She had a four o'clock appointment with the head of the Louvre bookshop, among other things.

None of this had anything to do with Mark, who would be a distraction. No thinking about sex while planning her future, it would just muddy things when she had to be absolutely clear in her head.

She explained this to him and he nodded in agreement, all reason. It didn't change his plans to stick by her all day, though.

But it turned out he wasn't a distraction. He was like...a superhero assistant who knew how to shut up.

He insisted on her sitting down to a warm breakfast,

politely not budging when she said she didn't have time. *Everyone has time for breakfast,* he said, and sat her down at a table in the glorious Ritz breakfast room. Turns out she did have time, after all.

She had a caffé crème, a warm croissant, a tiny plate of perfect scrambled eggs, and yogurt with homemade blueberry jam. It was perfect. Her closed stomach opened up and she knew instinctively that she'd face today better for having warm food in it.

When she stood, he put his hand to her back and walked her to the car and driver, who took her to her hotel where she quickly changed clothes. By the time they made it to the grand entrance of the Louvre, she was right on schedule and feeling good.

She walked to the glorious Pyramid, Mark at her side, and descended the escalator into the brightly illuminated space beneath it, happily breathing in the air of her favorite place in the world.

It was at the close-packed entrance that Mark was worth his weight in gold. He made sure they made their way steadily through the line of people with reserved tickets while also making sure that the energetic and enthusiastic crowds didn't impinge on her in any way. Harper got mildly claustrophobic in crowds, but not today.

Today they were through the stiles in no time. Security guards checked her bag and Mark's backpack and they were in the great hall in record time with minimum fuss.

Amazing.

Harper pulled out her map. She'd been to the Louvre many times but the huge building—the largest museum in the world —confused her every time.

She put the unfolded map on a side table, studying how to get to where she wanted to go.

Mark planted a big hand by the map. "Where are we going, honey?"

Whoa. She jumped at the endearment, blushing a little, then scolded herself for blushing.

"I want to make it to the Grande Galerie, where the Italian Renaissance paintings are. Where the *Mona Lisa* is, in a side room. We can look at it if you like. You're tall enough to see over the heads of the crowds. Have you seen it before?"

"Nope."

She smiled up at him. "You'll like it. If you get more than a glimpse, its mysterious beauty just shines through. At first you think it's just a dark and foggy portrait of a lady but it becomes much more than that. I hope you get a chance to see it properly." He probably would. Not only was he taller than most people, but he also knew how to create vital space around him.

She bent again over the map, trying to chart the fastest path to the Grande Galerie.

"Looking forward to it." He lay a big hand on her shoulder gently. "You can put that map away. We won't need it."

"What?" She frowned at him. "Of course we do. Didn't you say you'd never been to the Louvre before? It's a massive building. It's over 60,000 square meters. That's—" She paused, struggling with the figures.

"That's about 652,000 square feet." He was folding her map and tucking it into the side of her tote bag. "I know. But I studied the map and I'm pretty good with directions. I won't lead you astray."

The entrance to the Louvre was busy and confusing but Mark set off at a determined pace and as she followed him, she realized that he knew where he was going.

The terrible thing about orienting oneself in the Louvre was that there was stupendous artwork everywhere you looked and it scrambled the brains. Specifically, it scrambled the direction lobe in her brain.

It didn't scramble Mark's, though. He led them unerringly through the crowds up the spectacular grand staircase with a magnificent headless Nike at the landing.

Harper loved that statue and could stand gazing at it forever, at the elaborate wings and the folds of the peplum, at the grace and strength. Pure strong womanhood.

Winged Victory.

He had seen that she needed to stop and had somehow found a small corner of the landing that wasn't overwhelmed with people. Harper stared at the beautiful statue, mesmerized.

A young girl screamed with laughter and broke the spell. Harper had to shake her head and focus.

She looked up at her companion, feeling guilty. "If you've never been to the Louvre, it's a little overwhelming. Would you like me to give you a guided tour? Put some of the artworks in context for you?"

He dipped his head. "Nothing I'd like more. It would be an honor. But not today. Today is important to you, and you need to get your stuff done. That takes priority."

Of course, he was right. Something about the museum, which held a goodly portion of humanity's art, overloaded her neurons. She was hardwired to react to the artwork, but Mark was right. Not today. Today she had things to accomplish.

"Thanks," she said. "I sometimes get carried away and distracted. Like maybe you do at a plumbing supplies trade fair."

He smiled and said nothing. They continued on their way, Mark somehow making sure that they weren't crowded, magically evading the endless numbers of guided tours and student tours. It seemed everyone going up and down the spectacular staircase was excited but she and Mark seemed to move in a bubble of calm.

It was great.

When it became clear that Mark knew exactly where he

was going, she relaxed even further, starting to organize her thoughts, getting ready to take notes.

Even let her mind drift a little.

She was going to get a lot done today, she could feel it. Tomorrow, she had a meeting with a French printing company for a possible French edition of N/DESIGN. She was really revved for that. Everything was running smoothly, according to her plans and according to her dreams.

If she worked hard today she would be all caught up so there wouldn't be anything she had to do this evening except go out to dinner with Mark. Hoping he'd let her pay, though that seemed pretty farfetched from what she'd seen of him. He seemed to be pretty old school that way, not sitting down until she'd taken her seat, gently taking her elbow when they walked.

Like when he'd insisted on having his car and driver take her to her hotel after they'd deplaned. She would never have accepted ordinarily but there was a taxi strike and it was raining. He'd made his driver wait while he'd accompanied her to the taxi stand with no taxis and simply stood there while she looked in dismay at the teeming crowds fighting for places on buses into town.

Today he was somehow creating space around her in the crowded museum so she could work.

Unerringly, he guided her to the beginning of the Grande Galerie and, as it always did, it lifted her spirits. A large, long, vaulted portico with a glass ceiling, walls covered in paintings that were the pride of humanity. Any wall with ten paintings would have been enough for a museum in any other city. It was a priceless cornucopia of beauty spread out in lavish display, almost as far as the eye could see.

She could spend the entire day right here, and probably would have. By now she knew that Mark would stay quietly by her side and make sure she had water—she'd seen a couple of bottles of water in his backpack at the security station—and that no one disturbed her. He wouldn't complain and he wouldn't distract her. For some reason, she was absolutely sure about that.

She relaxed, aware now of how tense she'd been. She was walking a professional tightrope, about to leave a good job as assistant curator of a small but prestigious museum, for a flying leap into the unknown. Yet, for the first time, she was sure that it would work out.

At her side was a man she didn't know well, with whom she had nothing in common, but who pleased her.

She was going to get a lot of work done today, they were going to go out to dinner, and apparently there would be some more of that amazing sex on offer.

All in all, things were looking up. Life was pretty good.

"This place makes you happy," Mark said in a low, quiet voice.

She glanced up at him, startled. She wasn't used to the men in her life being perceptive about her moods. Men were mostly about their own moods.

"Why, yes. Yes, this place makes me very happy. I love it here."

"And you're happy about your project."

Harper blinked. "Are you a mind reader?"

His mouth curled up. "Maybe. Though no one has ever accused me of being capable of reading minds before. But you fascinate me, Harper Kendall."

Harper's mouth opened and closed. She had no idea what to say.

Mark touched her shoulder. "Sorry. I promised myself I wouldn't distract you. We're at the Grand Gallery and you have work to do." He lifted his palm. "It's all fascinating. I'll just walk beside you and take it all in."

"We can—" Harper took a deep breath. It felt like she was

taking a plunge. "We can come back sometime. Day after tomorrow, if you want. So you can see things at your pace."

Wow. It was a rule for her, not to talk about the future until the fourth or fifth date. No entanglements in the beginning was her mantra. And here she was, offering to take him around the Louvre some other day.

The smile dropped from his face and he looked at her intently. "I'd like that. I'd really like that."

O-kay.

A small commitment further along than dinner tonight had been made. Oddly, she didn't feel trapped or hemmed in.

Well, she was here for a reason, might as well get to it. She pulled out her Florentine marbleized paper notebook, easier for taking notes on the fly than any electronic device.

Mark stood slightly behind her, to the side. Standing completely still, never fidgeting, patient and solid.

He looked so...so sane. So reliable. And, well, hot.

She hesitated for just a second, and then told him her plans. No one else in the world knew except for her future partners, not even her parents. The art and design world was small and she and her partners had planned the launch of the magazine with the secrecy of those planning D-Day.

But she wanted this man to know. To know her plans, to know *her.*

"Um, I have some plans." His gaze honed in on her face, as if he instinctively knew she was talking about something important to her. His gaze never wavered.

"Leaving the boss from hell." Mark's deep voice was grim.

Well, Ivan wasn't that bad... Yes, he was, she decided. He was petty and vindictive and hated talented workers. He was awful. "Absolutely. Leaving the boss from hell." She smiled at the thought.

"I don't know much about design, but I'd bet you anything you want that the project will be successful. What's the plan?"

"I have three partners and we're planning on founding a new design magazine. The online version will be interactive." She turned to the wall of magnificent paintings. "I want to go out in style, so my last article for my museum's magazine will be how elements of fantasy in artwork presaged changes in the way people were going to live. Some deep chord in humanity only rings for the creative mind, attuned to the coming changes."

It was something deeply hidden in humans and it fascinated her.

Mark's gaze never left her face.

"Take, for example, color on walls. Medieval paintings often have walls that are colored red and yellow, yet most walls at that time were whitewashed. Mainly because whitewash is a disinfectant and there were epidemics of cholera, diphtheria, even pockets of plague at regular intervals. People saw white walls every day of their lives, yet paintings started depicting richly colored walls, something that was not to be a regular feature in homes for another couple hundred years."

Color as stimulant, she wrote in the notebook. The hook on which she would hang the article.

As she made her way from painting to painting, she was dimly aware of Mark. He kept out of her way, out of even her line of sight, as if he didn't want to distract her at all. Nobody distracted her. In the crowded rooms full of enthusiastic art lovers, bored gaggles of school kids, dutiful tourists ticking off a major attraction, no one bothered her. No one invaded her space. She was able to...*wander* from painting to painting, and it was smooth and painless.

Thanks to Mark.

She was almost at the end of her notebook. Thank God she had three more just like it. This was so exciting. The article was going to write itself and it would be her ticket out from under the sharp claws of Ivan. It was going to work. It was going to *rock*.

The next side room held the *Mona Lisa*. She was sure Mark would enjoy it. And it was sort of a litmus test. A lot of people saw a very small, very dark portrait of a woman who wasn't beautiful by modern standards. A lot of people were disappointed when they saw it.

Everyone took photos because...well, the *Mona Lisa*. You had to show that you'd been there. But not everyone understood it or appreciated it. It would be interesting to get Mark's take.

She smiled up at him. "You're being really patient. Thanks. Now you get your treat. In that room is the—"

She stopped, mouth open. There'd been a loud booming noise with a background tinkling. And now staccato noises. What—

Harper found herself slammed against the Gallery wall, Mark leaning against her so hard she found it hard to breath. His arms were against the wall, head bent over hers, shielding her.

She looked up, alarmed. His face had lost that bland, pleasant look. He looked hard, features pulled tight.

The staccato sounds were getting closer and she could hear screams.

"Mark, what's happening?" she whispered.

Other people in the Grand Gallery were milling, starting to get agitated. The screams and ripping sounds came ever closer.

"Unless I miss my guess, that was the Pyramid blowing up." He spoke without looking at her, head swiveling as he took in the crowds, close to panic. "And those are AK-47s. The Louvre is under attack."

5

G*oddamn!*

It was a terrorist attack! This was the kind of thing he'd trained all his adult life to handle, but right now he was hamstrung. Mark had Harper to protect and he was fucking *unarmed.*

He lifted his head, listening closely. There was no way to tell how many attackers there were but they were running. And shooting. And killing. The ripping sound of machine gun fire was punctuated by the screams of the wounded and the dying.

Mark consulted his inner map. Right now, a pack of terrorists was running up that monumental staircase, maybe the forerunners were at the top of the stairs by now.

The tourists in the huge Gallery were panicking outright, running away from the sounds of violence toward the other end of the Gallery, the exit. Perfectly normal behavior for untrained civilians. But the exit from the Gallery wasn't the exit from the building. They were far from anywhere they could get out of the building.

The shots were coming closer. Mark did not want to be caught in the big open space when they arrived. They were sitting ducks. But there was nowhere to hide. All the rooms were large, open, without any furniture except a few benches. Nothing that could remotely be considered concealment.

There were more screams now. Whoever was attacking was mowing tourists down by the dozens. Separate guns could be heard. Mark estimated at least twenty separate firearms.

Fuck.

Suddenly, shots were coming from the other end of the Gallery. A pincer movement, carefully planned. Good tactics, all things considered. It would take a battalion to conquer the Louvre, as big as it was. These terrorists were aiming to isolate the Grand Gallery, containing the most famous painting in the world, the *Mona Lisa*.

"Mark?" He looked down at a shaken Harper, white-faced but not panicking like the other tourists. "What's happening?"

Mark didn't answer for a second. He studied the big room just off the gallery, one of a series of ten.

He peered harder and saw a thin line in the wall, barely visible.

He held her by the shoulders. "We don't have much time, honey. I think I see a door in this room." He pointed with his chin at the large side room. "Is that possible? The walls are thick. Are there chambers between the walls?"

"Ye-yes. It's where supplies were stored during the construction of the building. But they're locked, Mark."

It was all he needed to know. There was maximum confusion at both ends of the long Gallery and tourists had fled from the side rooms. "Let's go."

She followed without question. Mark felt a punch of... something, somewhere in the vicinity of his heart. She was so shocked her face was white, eyes enormous, pupils dilated. This was completely outside anything she could possibly have encountered in life.

And yet, shocked and frightened, she was following his

lead. His woman was following his lead. He'd found her and he could lose her any minute.

They had seconds.

Mark was pulling out his little toolkit from his backpack.

His packs, whether a normal one for urban life or his mission backpack, were always packed a certain way and he knew how to instantly put his hands on what he needed. What he needed was his lock-pick set, and he found it immediately. The lock-pick set was miniature and highly effective.

He quickly walked Harper over to the hairline opening in the wall, lock-pick set in hand. "How many people know about these doors?"

"Not many, I imagine." She turned her ashen, stricken face up to his, then looked at his hands. But her voice was calm. "You'd have to be an architectural historian, I guess."

Which she was.

"We're going to have to chance it," Mark said as the door opened. "Hurry, honey."

Her eyes widened, but she scrambled inside and he pulled the door closed just as the sounds of the attack breached the Gallery.

The terrorists were here.

Mark switched on the flashlight function of his cellphone.

"That won't last long," Harper whispered in a shaky voice.

"I have several high-performance rechargers," he whispered back, most of his attention on studying the space they were in. It was intramural space, about four feet wide. It was high enough for oxygen not to be a problem and he saw that it followed the walls. To his left, it took a dogleg. On the other side was the eastern wall of the Salle des Etats, the *Mona Lisa* room.

The floor was dusty and the air felt dead, but it was a good hiding place.

"Here," he said. "Take this." He handed Harper a small but

powerful flashlight. Without the cellphone and the flashlight, they'd be in pitch darkness. Civilians panicked without light. For Spec Ops soldiers, though, darkness was cover.

He himself preferred darkness, as long as the enemy was in darkness too.

"Shine it upward and make sure you don't direct it toward the door. The door is beveled and the seams are tight but we can't take chances."

"Okay," she said, her voice firmer. "Thanks. I don't know anyone else who'd bring a flashlight to a museum, but this is really great. What else do you have in your magic backpack?"

She was trying to joke but he was dead serious when he answered. "Enough food and water to stay alive for at least two days, light and a way to keep track of what's going on. I think we're going to be under siege."

"Good. Excellent. You were a Boy Scout, right?"

Mark flashed her a grin. He was so proud of her. One thing he'd learned on countless missions was that the make-or-break element in surviving wasn't just having top-tier gear and training, but your attitude. Keeping your head was key. She was keeping hers.

They were going to survive this.

With some help.

They walked around the corner of the great room until they came to the wall of the Salle des Etats. He placed a tiny instrument that looked vaguely like a stethoscope against the wall. It amplified and clarified sounds.

Shots. Screams. Shouts.

Mark closed his eyes, concentrating on the shouts. Two men, barking orders. He listened carefully. The Salle des Etats with the *Mona Lisa* was to become their headquarters.

Two voices, one deep, one lighter, shouting commands. The accent was Syrian. Other voices out in the Gallery shouted in broken English and French. Herding the tourists into the Salle des Etats.

From far away on the left and the right came the sounds of drilling. The deep voice said that the entire Gallery was closed off now, at both ends. They were locking themselves in. Mark was right. It was a siege situation.

He'd heard what was going on. Now to see.

He pulled out a tiny but powerful and silent drill. He ran his flashlight over the wall that was part of the *Mona Lisa* room and settled on a spot where a corner was formed between the side wall and the back wall, five inches from the floor.

He crouched and applied the drill. Harper crouched beside him, holding the flashlight. She'd discovered that the light's intensity could be regulated by twisting the handle and had dimmed the light to the lowest setting. Mark could see enough to work by but didn't have to worry about light accidentally shining through the hole he was drilling.

"Thanks," he whispered.

She nodded, watching him carefully. "I don't know what you're doing but you're going to need light to do it by."

The drill ate through the wall silently, all detritus falling on their side of the wall. Mark sent up a silent thanks to the engineers who'd made the drill. Once the drill head made it through the wall, it stopped instantly. Mark knew from experience that it wouldn't jut out but would be flush with the wall, to all intents and purposes completely invisible.

He pulled out a cable from the other end of the drill and connected it to his cell. Then he pulled out wired earbuds, again fitting the end to the cellphone. He offered one earbud to Harper and she leaned in close, shiny hair swinging over her shoulder, giving off a little burst of lemon scent.

Oh God, the smell of her hair was so wonderful in this ancient, dusty place that felt like a tomb. He looked at her, just a glance. She met his gaze and the electricity of that rocked him. For just a moment, it was if they were one person.

Mark pressed a button and his screen came alive, a wide-angle-lens view of the room, complete with sound. Like a movie from hell.

The man with the deep voice was squat, powerful, the leader. Though black-haired, his skin was very fair. Maybe some Iranian blood there. He was directing his men to stand against the walls, three to a wall, and Mark could see that at least two men were stationed at the wide entry to the room, backs to them, weapons trained outward. Mark could take it as a given that there were other terrorists stationed along the Gallery.

What they saw on his cell screen was bloodcurdling. At least a hundred tourists were sitting on the floor, hands on their heads, some bleeding, all terrified. And the men holding their guns trained on them, holding them hostage, were dressed in French police uniforms.

Which explained how they'd managed the initial attack.

"Youssef," the leader shouted. "How many out there?"

"The leader is asking how many dead are out in the Gallery." Mark spoke in a very low voice, barely audible.

"You speak Arabic?" Harper asked, shocked. Instinctively, she followed his lead. Not whispering but murmuring.

He nodded. "Yeah. One of the guys in the corridor, guarding the *Mona Lisa* room, said there were fifty people down. He said about twenty were wounded and couldn't walk." He met her eyes. "Gunshot wounds are dangerous. If they don't allow medical personnel in immediately—and they won't—the wounded out there are going to die."

Her eyes searched his before dropping back to the screen. "I think a lot of people have already died. They shot their way here."

Mark nodded, and went back to watching and listening

carefully. He hadn't told Harper that most of the tourists out in the Gallery were dead. Those inside the room were cowed, many bloody and bruised. One little girl started wailing, terrified and bleeding from a cut on her forehead.

She attracted the attention of the leader, who scowled at her and her mother. The mother gathered the little girl to her, trying to hush her.

"Shut up!" the leader shouted in Arabic. The girl sobbed in her mother's arms.

The girl's sobbing made the crowd on the floor restless. Humans—normal humans—are programmed to respond to a child's cries. There was a rustling noise. Two men placed their hands on the ground, preparatory to getting up.

"Shut up! *Tais toi!*" one of the guards shouted. The fact that he was dressed in a police uniform and was speaking both English and French made them hesitate. But the little girl didn't care how he was dressed or what he spoke. She responded instinctively to the brutality she must have sensed in him.

"Make her shut up," the leader said in Arabic.

"He's given an order to shut the little girl up." Mark tensed.

The man dressed in the police uniform pointed his gun at the girl and the mother screamed, throwing herself over her daughter.

The man pulled her off the little girl, hauled back his booted foot and kicked the girl, hard. So hard she was lifted off the ground. She crumpled to the ground and lay still.

Mark rose, enraged.

"No!" Harper clutched at his arm, pulling him back down. "You'll only endanger yourself and not help them. Please, Mark, please." She spoke low but urgently.

Mark trembled. Technically, he could open the door, run into the next room and tackle the fuckhead, but Harper was right. What would he accomplish? He'd be mowed down.

Mark had faced death many times and he wasn't afraid of

dying. On the other hand, dying like an idiot, facing twelve armed men unarmed, was the mark of a fool.

And worse. He'd leave Harper undefended.

But it was hard, sinking back into a crouch and watching his cell screen. Watching terrorists hold innocent people at gunpoint. Watching a man kick a child. Knowing that these men had shot and killed their way to this point.

"Mark," Harper murmured, putting her hand over his where he was clutching the cell so hard the plastic crackled.

He blew out a breath, loosened his hold.

She stroked his hand, trying to get him to calm down. "I tried to call the police. The 9-1-1 number in France—everywhere in Europe—is 1-1-2. But I couldn't make the call. It wouldn't connect."

The rage was slowly subsiding in Mark's head. Cold mission awareness took its place. "They're using a jammer. They've got hundreds of hostages and each one has a cell. The first thing they'd need to do is create uncertainty." He dug into his backpack. "But this is a satphone and doesn't use cell towers."

She gave a little gasp of surprise. "Excellent! Call 1-1-2!"

"Not yet. Not calling the police." Mark punched in the first number on speed dial and inserted a separate earbud. "Some of the terrorists are dressed in French police uniforms. They have an inside guy. Maybe several. Yo." He sat up as he heard his COO's voice. It was 5 a.m. back in Boston but Mike sounded awake and alert. "Mike. Code Red. I'm in the Louvre. It's under attack by about twelve tangos that I know of. More in the building, probably many more. They're holding over a hundred hostages in the Grand Gallery, in the *Mona Lisa* room; there are more wounded and dead tourists out in the corridor. AK-47s. Each tango has about ten mags and several have suicide vests."

He felt more than saw Harper look up at him in shock. She hadn't recognized them but he had.

"More tangos are outside the room and they're laying explosives. Several had backpacks."

He'd seen two terrorists out in the wide corridor pressing C4 between the floor and the wall just before he'd closed the door.

"Are you safe?" Mike asked.

"For the moment, yes, we're safe."

A slight pause as Mike processed the *we*. "There's no chatter on this yet."

Mark glanced at the cell screen. "They'll contact the outside world. They'll have demands. They have hostages."

"Agreed. Implicitly, they also have the most famous work of art in the world. I have a friend high up in French law enforcement."

"Careful, Mike. Like I said, some of the tangos have police uniforms. There's some kind of leak there. A mole. Maybe several."

"Okay. I'll get back to you soonest." The connection cut off.

Mark studied the screen, the dynamics. The hostages were crowded together in the immense room. Nine tangos with AK-47s pointed at them, another two at the huge entrance to the room, AK-47s pointed outward.

The men, women and children sitting on the floor were terrified. After seeing what happened to the little girl, the children were muted, stifling their sobs.

Mark saw the little girl, unmoving, her mother silently crying over her still little body. She was alive, though. Breathing shallowly, that small torso moving up and down. He watched the man who'd kicked her so viciously, dressed in a police uniform, marking his face carefully.

That man would pay. They all would.

Harper was seated against the wall, the dimmed flashlight placed on the floor next to her. It heightened her features, highlighting the high cheekbones, the full mouth, the long lashes.

She was holding her knees with trembling hands, but she was keeping it together.

"A siege," she said.

"We're okay," Mark bent to murmur in her ear. "I have enough water to last two days. Three actually. I can go without water for long periods. I have some protein bars for food. We just have to hang tight."

Okay. She mouthed the word rather than say it.

He drew back a moment to look her in the eyes. She was scared but functional. Of course she was scared, she'd have to be crazy not to be scared.

A few inches of wall separated them from terrorists who'd already killed God knew how many people. Mark had dealt with crazed fanatics all his adult life. He knew that they'd kill them without a second thought.

Mark placed a hand over her linked hands, letting her feel his strength and warmth, which would do more to reassure her than words could ever do. But she'd need the words, too.

He placed his mouth against her ear again and breathed in her scent, this woman who was precious to him.

"It will be okay. As long as I'm alive, you will be fine. And I'm a hard man to kill." He couldn't resist dropping a kiss on her hair.

Her hands flexed under his, one of her thumbs curling around his hand. She nodded.

Mark shifted to sit next to her, back against the wall, legs bent. He put his arm around her shoulders and she dropped her head to his chest.

There wasn't much he could do right now. Outside this wall he was badly outnumbered and completely outgunned. Mike would be working it. Everything he could do, he would do. But for now, it was a waiting game.

He had no weapons. But they had water and food and for

the moment, a secure location. Harper was safe and would stay that way.

"Mark?" She was keeping her voice so low he wouldn't have heard her a foot away.

"Yeah?"

She looked up at him, searching his eyes. "You speak Arabic. You come prepared for a siege of the Louvre. You've got scars all over. You're not a plumbing supplies importer, are you?"

He tucked a lock of soft, shiny hair behind her ear and kissed her cheek.

"No."

6

What a foolish question. Whatever Mark Redmond was, he wasn't a bland businessman.

Harper would have been angry that he'd lied to her except for the fact that because he was what he was—whatever that was—she wasn't lying outside in the Grand Gallery in a pool of her own blood.

He'd instantly recognized what was happening and, with seconds to spare, had found them shelter and concealment. She knew about the spaces between the walls but she'd been too shocked to even think of it.

He'd not only known what to do, but he'd had survival basics in his backpack, including a set of lock picks.

Lock picks. Hmm. "You're not an international thief hoping to steal a painting, are you?"

He smiled, deep grooves bracketing his mouth. God, when he smiled, he become so insanely attractive...and what was wrong with her that she was thinking of that right now?

"Nope. Not an international thief. One of the good guys."

Harper nodded. Yes. He was one of the good guys. "Military?"

"Former," he nodded. "Now private security. I have my own company."

She sighed. A former soldier, now into private security. *So* not her type, yet here she was. He'd saved her life, he'd given her the best sex she'd ever had and, more surprisingly, she liked him. A lot.

More than liked him.

"Not your style, huh?" His strong, heavy arm curled around her shoulders. He caressed her cheek with his forefinger.

"Right now, you're exactly my style."

"Damn right." The smile dropped from his face and his features grew tight. "I told you, as long as I am alive, nothing will happen to you."

It was crazy. There were terrorists with machine guns mere feet from them. Mark wasn't armed. The security measures at the entrance under the Pyramid had been too strong for that. Of course, bad things could still happen to her. He was tall and strong and smart and apparently knew how to handle himself in dangerous situations, but he wasn't Superman.

And yet...and yet. She was terrified and not terrified at the same time. They were in the middle of a massive terrorist attack, the biggest she'd ever heard of except for 9/11. It had sounded as if the terrorists had *swarmed* in, armed and blood-thirsty. If they discovered her and Mark's hiding place, a pull of the trigger and they'd both be dead in a second.

But Mark was smart and knew what he was doing. There was a possibility he could keep them safe if he could stop himself from doing something brave and foolish. She'd recognized the tension in him when the terrorist had viciously kicked the little girl. Every muscle in his body had been screaming at him to go out there and defend the child. She could see it. But he'd controlled himself.

The expression on his face had been terrifying. Muscles

tense, eyes cold, and a distinct air of violence around him. She wasn't scared of him. But the terrorists should be.

No, though Mark Redmond was turning out to be something far more dangerous than a businessman, from some deep well of knowledge inside her, she knew beyond a shadow of a doubt that he would die defending her.

So, yes. Maybe they would make it out alive, even if those poor people huddled on the floor in the *Mona Lisa* room wouldn't.

"How did the terrorists get in past security?" she asked.

Security everywhere was tight nowadays, even in museums. She'd been shocked at the security measures at the entrance to the museum. She hadn't been to the Louvre for three years and things were much tighter now. They'd carefully checked her purse and she'd had to walk through a metal detector.

It still shocked her. She remembered the first time there had been security checks in a museum and she'd been dumbfounded. Who would want to attack a *museum*?

Judging by today, lots of people.

Mark bent closer and she was almost ashamed that his voice in her ear gave her goose bumps. Not fear goose bumps. The other kind. "Remember that a lot of them are dressed as police officers. That's how they managed. Either they're simply wearing uniforms, or worse, they really are cops. Infiltrated into the system. They'd have seen to it that the weapons passed through security."

She looked at him, nudging his thigh with her knee. "They didn't catch on to your magic backpack with the lock pick. Anything else in there they should have caught?"

"Yeah. A very sharp ceramic knife in my boot and I have a combat baton. Plus some detcord and a small amount of explosives."

Her breath caught. "Really?"

"Really."

"But that—that's—"

"Illegal? Yeah. Useful? Yeah."

She thought about the *Mona Lisa* room, the poor miserable tourists huddled in the middle, surrounded by gunmen. "I don't think explosives would be useful in this particular situation."

"You're right. The room is too big. But you never know. Better to have it and not need it than need it and not have it."

She turned to him, looked him straight in the eyes. "The first priority is the safety of those poor hostages. But the paintings in that room—they are invaluable. Part of humanity's heritage. And the *Mona Lisa...*" She covered her mouth in horror at the thought of the artwork, of the *Mona Lisa*, being destroyed.

Mark nodded, then frowned. He'd been keeping an eye on the screen. He tapped his ear, which she understood to turn the cellphone audio on, and angled the screen so they could both watch.

"They're dragging something into the room."

Harper's heart skipped a beat. "Explosives?"

"No," he murmured, eyes glued to the screen. He tilted his head then sucked in a breath. "I knew it."

"What?" she mouthed.

"Camera and a tripod," Mark said, his mouth a thin line. He shot her a glance then went back to watching the screen intently. She looked down, too.

Camera. Tripod.

Oh, dear God.

Harper dug her fingers into Mark's strong shoulder, so hard she'd hurt a lesser man. She knew what was coming next.

The leader took a collapsible stool and positioned it under the *Mona Lisa*.

Two of the attackers brought out a bright green sheet with

Arabic writing in black and held it as a backdrop, right under the *Mona Lisa*.

"What does the writing say?"

Mark waited until the sheet was fully extended. He sighed softly, hanging his head for a moment. "Surah 47."

She looked at him, waiting.

The muscles of his jaw worked. "When you encounter an unbeliever, strike him at the neck."

Harper's eyes widened in horror. "You mean—"

"Yeah." He gave a jerky nod. "Behead him."

They stared at each other wordlessly, then dropped their eyes back down to the screen. The leader was sitting on the stool and began a chant in Arabic.

The leader started sliding slightly right or left on the stool, according to the signs made by the man staring down into the camera. Finally, they got the position to their liking.

Insanely bizarre. They were behaving like amateur film-makers, making sure they got the best shots possible, as if they weren't monsters who'd left a trail of blood behind them.

The leader started speaking, voice low at first. Then, he worked himself up into a screaming rage, spittle flying from his mouth. Finally he stopped and, incredibly, smiled at the cameraman. The cameraman smiled back, holding up a thumb. The universal symbol for approval.

The leader stood up, grabbed a small bottle of water from a backpack lying on the floor, finished it in three long gulps, then sat back down again.

Mark put his lips to her ear. "I think he's going to repeat what he just said in Arabic. He'll speak either English or French. If he speaks French, can you translate for me? I want to know if he says the same thing he said in Arabic."

"Sure." She fit one earbud into her ear.

They watched as the leader shouted a few orders at the men

lining the walls. One of the men walked forward. Mark manipulated the screen until the focus was on the man, who reached down and pulled a pretty young woman up by her long honey-blonde hair. She screamed, terrified.

A young man, tall and gangly, dressed in a tee shirt and shorts, stood up instantly, shouting "Let her go!"

The leader made a casual gesture with his hand and one of the terrorists behind the young man lifted the butt of his rifle and brought it down hard on the young man's head.

He fell to the floor instantly, as if he were a puppet whose strings had been cut. Harper stifled a sob. No one could hear her in the room. People were screaming, the leader was screaming. But she understood that their lives depended on no one knowing they were in here so she swallowed her horror.

Mark's arm around her tightened. "He didn't shoot that boy. That's something."

Harper nodded, not trusting her voice.

Pandemonium in the room, everyone's eyes on the young boy and the pretty girl. The boy lay face down, blond hair bloody. But his feet and hands were working. He was alive.

The leader lifted his gun and shot a couple of bullets into the ceiling. The room instantly quieted.

"We are going to record a message the whole world will be seeing. The next one to make noise will be shot. Do you understand?" he said in French and then English.

Harper translated. The hostages on the floor were quiet, frozen. Even the children.

The leader put down his gun and lifted a huge sword. It looked like a ceremonial sword but it also gleamed. It was a working sword. Harper glanced up at Mark's grim face. His expression was hard and cold as he watched the screen.

The leader pulled a balaclava over his head and nodded to the camera operator on the other side of the huge room. The operator had his back to the huge painting *The Wedding Feast at*

Cana. The leader had his back to the *Mona Lisa.* And Harper had no doubt that he'd artfully framed his shot of the scene that would be seen around the world. The terrorist clad in black, faceless, holding a young woman by her long blonde hair, behind him poetry inciting to a beheading, above that the most famous painting in the world.

A real marketing coup for the insane terrorist brand.

The leader started talking and Harper translated as he spoke.

"Attention France! We are your sons, and we reject you and everything you stand for! You are an immoral people, an abomination in the eyes of God. He will smite you through us. You are holding warriors for justice in your prisons. Fourteen of them. Here are their names."

Harper stopped translating as the man read out names. Many Arabic names, some with either a French first name or last name.

"Our brothers in arms will be freed from your unjust imprisonment immediately. We have one hundred and twelve infidels in this room. Not to mention the obscene and immoral painting behind me."

He turned slightly so whoever was watching could not mistake his meaning. Two of his men had taken down the Plexiglas shield in front of the *Mona Lisa* so it was unprotected.

"We have also planted explosives throughout this building full of immoral and obscene depictions of depravity. If our brothers in arms are not freed within twenty-four hours, the people in this room will die, one by one, this building will be destroyed and—"

The man kept his fist in the young woman's hair, turned and slashed at the *Mona Lisa*, leaving a ten-inch gash across the neck. If the *Mona Lisa* had been a person instead of a painting, she would have been beheaded.

There was a collective gasp in the room, audible even

through the earbuds. Harper was terrified for the poor tourists under a death threat. But there was also something coldly evil about the desecration of one of the most beautiful works of art in human history.

The terrorist understood full well the power of the slashing of the *Mona Lisa*. When he turned back to the camera, his dark eyes were glittering with triumph, knowing that the entire world would see what he'd done.

"If you try to storm the building, we will kill ten hostages for every martyr brother killed. Free our warriors or we will bring down this building with all its abominations."

With a gesture of contempt, the terrorist let go of the young woman's hair and she fell to the ground weeping. He panned the room, sword held high, the other terrorists around the room with guns pointed at the terrified hostages.

Everyone was still and silent except for the weeping woman, crawling to the young man who'd defended her.

Mark put his mouth to her ear. "That was different from what he said in Arabic, which was a call to arms. This was the first salvo in hostage negotiations. What was his French like?"

"Perfect," Harper said, turning her head to brush her lips against his ear. Her nose was close enough to his cheek to feel the slight bite of his beard. His skin was warm, rough. His smell was familiar. She'd had her face against his skin all last night.

A bloom of heat shot through her, a cruel and inappropriate reaction of her body that had nothing to do with *her*. She felt as if he'd hijacked her body, so it responded helplessly to the smell of his skin, the rough feel of his beard.

"Native speaker?" he asked, and she had to wrench her mind back to their awful reality.

"Yes." Harper nodded. "Native speaker, probably Parisian. Not very educated French, though. A couple of grammatical errors."

Mark nodded, pulling out his satphone. He switched earbuds and tapped the new one once.

"Hey," he said. "Sitrep. There's going to be a video released soon. Guy's recorded a hostage video, which he delivered in French, in a mask. But I have footage of him before he put on the mask, when he recorded another video in Arabic. I'm sure he's in some database, so have someone do a facial recog. Speaks Arabic with a slight foreign accent, speaks French like a native. The Arabic video is a call to arms. The French video is blackmail. Free prisoner friends or we will shoot the hostages and blow up the Louvre. The prisoners are mentioned by name. They are probably in the La Santé Prison. Get in touch with our contacts at DGSE because the French police are compromised."

Harper couldn't hear anything bleeding out from his earbud as he listened. Then he nodded.

"Copy that. These guys aren't joking. I think the Louvre is full of dead bodies and I think they really do have it rigged to blow. Tell the head of the DGSE that I'm here. Use me."

He thumbed the connection off.

"Um, Mark?"

He'd been lost in thought for a moment after speaking with his teammate, but when he turned his head to look at her it was like being hit with a spotlight, his attention was so intense.

"I'm not a communications expert, but don't you think they might be monitoring cellphone and even satphone usage? They told all the hostages to throw their phones on the floor and that they'd know if they tried to use them. Could they trace us through one of your phones?"

I don't think the CIA knows about this frequency, let alone those people out there."

Okay, that made her feel better. "So, what are we going to do?"

He settled against the wall and put his arm back around her shoulders. God, it felt so good to lean against him. He felt more solid than the wall. She leaned her head against his shoulder.

"Do?" He dropped his head back against the wall. "For now, we wait."

7

Soldiers have to know how to burst into action in a second. They also have to know how to wait. Mark was one of those soldiers who knew how to wait. He'd once waited three days for a shot at an ISIS commander. He hadn't eaten, he'd drunk very sparingly because he'd had to piss himself where he lay, and he hadn't slept.

But he'd gotten the job done.

There was nothing he could do right now, not until Mike got back to him. He couldn't take on armed terrorists in a large room, unarmed. And he didn't know how many were on sentry duty in the Gallery. He didn't want to get himself killed and he didn't want to leave Harper undefended. Not going to happen.

So now it was a waiting game.

They had water and some food. They were safely in hiding. Mark knew that as soon as that video hit the media, the entire French antiterrorism force would crank into gear immediately. The DGSE was staffed with smart, tough guys, backed by a smart and tough intelligence community.

A lot would have to happen before the terrorists blew up the Louvre. They had time.

And he was with Harper, which wasn't a hardship.

She was sitting hip to hip beside him, her head on his shoulder, but she wasn't freaking and she wasn't panicking. Smart as she was, she understood the danger, but she was keeping it together.

"So...what else is in the magic backpack? Besides a lock pick, enough water to withstand a siege and a special phone that has its own cellular network?" she asked, voice low.

"Well..." Mark reached out to pull the backpack toward him. He picked it up and rapped his knuckles against the back. It gave a low *pock* sound. "Bulletproof plate. Like having half a tactical vest. No guns because I can't travel with them, and I knew they wouldn't let me into the Louvre armed anyway. But I have that baton I told you about. You can defend yourself pretty well with a baton in close-quarters battle."

She tucked a shiny lock of hair behind her ear. "Show me."

Mark took out a small metal cylinder, pressed a button, and a long baton popped out soundlessly. Mark ran his hand from the handle up to the tip. "Stainless steel. Can break bones easily. I have one at home that also delivers an electric shock like a cattle prod. Very handy."

She shook her head. "If you're up against someone armed, I guess you're out of luck."

"In theory, yes. If you're smart and fast, you can use the element of surprise. It's a good impact weapon."

"Beats my pepper spray." She always kept a full bottle of pepper spray in her purse.

He swiveled his head. "You ever use your spray?"

"Actually, yes. At the end of a date from hell. He worked in a bank and I thought he was safe, but..."

"He wasn't," Mark said grimly.

Harper shivered at the memory. "No."

He clenched his fists. "I hate the thought of some suit trying to hurt you. I'm sorry that happened to you."

She made a small noise in her throat and looked up at him. It was amazing how beautiful she looked even in the harsh shadows of the up-light of the flashlight. It was meant to show details and it was hard light. Yet it loved her face, caressed it. Highlighted the graceful jawline, high cheekbones, smooth forehead.

In a cramped, dusty, airless storage space, turning stuffy, she was immensely precious. He kept his face expressionless but if he ever found out the name of that fucker who worked in a bank and tried to hurt her, he'd rip his head off.

Mark kept one eye on the cell screen, watching what was unfolding in the room. The leader was agitated. This was a large-scale attack on one of the most famous buildings in the world. They had their goal and had stated it but the leader would understand that as soon as that video hit the media, they'd be surrounded by the largest law-enforcement deployment in France's history. Though the leader held most of the cards, some of them were wild cards.

There were over a hundred hostages in the room being held by twelve armed men. If those hundred hostages had been former Rangers or SEALs or Deltas, the guard dogs wouldn't stand a chance. No twelve men could hold a hundred Spec Ops warriors. But the hostages were women and children and untrained men.

Still, you never knew. In that group could be some dangerous men, like himself. And though the terrorists were armed and the hostages weren't, a hundred people were a lot of people to keep an eye on.

Fuckhead was in charge right now, an armed fanatic who was presumably prepared to die a martyr, and he could make good on his promise to shoot the hostages one by one. On live TV.

French soldiers could lay siege but no siege would withstand a dead body an hour. Not to mention the fact that the leader would choose pretty young women and children to shoot. On camera. These kinds of men were merciless and never missed a trick.

Right now, the leader was pacing the perimeter of the room, speaking with his men.

Nothing was happening and Mark guessed that nothing would until the video was released and someone in authority set up comms, or tried to.

One of the terrorists pulled something out of a backpack. A laptop. Two laptops. He opened them up and set one to France1, the main French news station, and the other to CNN. They were expecting the news to hit at any moment.

Five men surrounded the laptops, jabbering excitedly in a mixture of Syrian Arabic and Iraqi Marsh Arabic. Their guard was down. Mark could have taken them down if he had his old team with him. But he didn't. Going after them single-handedly would just get him killed and would leave Harper alone.

The Moscow theater hostage crisis lasted 4 days. The Beslan school siege lasted 3 days. This hostage crisis, though in a country that wasn't willing to sacrifice hostages, could last days, weeks. If Mark went out and sacrificed himself, Harper would be left to starve or die of thirst before it ended.

He had a few ideas but they would have to wait.

"So," Harper said, looking up at him. "A plumbing supplies importer?"

He looked at her and smiled.

"How did you come up with that?"

"It's the most boring job I could think of. Actually, my dad had a plumbing supplies import business. A really big one. I could bore you senseless comparing French and Italian zinc tubing. The job is the kiss of death. No one wants to hear about it. Another boring job is tax software manager."

"You've used that one, as well?"

Mark nodded. "And logistics expert a couple of times. That's a big yawn, too."

She put a hand on his chest, her fingers finding the knot of tissue that was a bullet scar and he'd told her was from a practice stick. "Those scars are not from practicing martial arts in dojos."

"Nope."

They sat in silence for a few moments.

"So...who are you? I could make a couple of educated guesses. And if you are what I think you are, you probably can't say much. But the truth is that we could die here. We've...been to bed together. I think I deserve to know who you really are."

They *had* had sex, and Mark wanted to have sex with her again. And again and again. But it wasn't just that. He wanted to simply spend time with her. She was so beautiful, so graceful and so very smart. Every minute with her was a pleasure, and he wanted a lot of those minutes. So if they were going to be together, yes, she deserved to know who he was.

But it went against his every instinct to tell her the truth. He hadn't told anyone outside the service and his business who he really was for years. His company employed two anti-social media experts who worked night and day to keep him and his business out of the news. He operated best in the dark. He hadn't been photographed other than for IDs since he was 22. Revealing his identity was almost like slicing open his chest and showing his beating heart. His throat felt tight.

When he didn't say anything, Harper looked down at her hands. "Is Mark Redmond even your real name?"

His throat opened up a little. "Yes."

"Well, that's a start."

This was surprisingly hard. Being naked with her, with all his scars, was nothing in comparison. Mark didn't know how to continue. Foreign territory. He'd never opened up to anyone, ever. The people he worked with knew who he was, what he could do. The rest of humanity stayed in the dark.

Once he started, though, it became easier. Sitting with his back against a dusty wall, not knowing if they'd live to see another day, with murderous terrorists on the other side of the wall, he told this beautiful woman who fascinated him the truth.

"I wasn't brilliant at school, but I loved military history, had excellent hand-eye coordination and was really good at martial arts, which made the military an obvious choice. I think my dad would have wanted me to take over his business—boring as it was when he retired but it was clear to him by the time I was ten that wasn't going to happen. What I said about the dojo was mostly true. I *have* been around dojos since I was a kid. I swept and changed towels at my first dojo in exchange for some lessons. My dad didn't want to pay for them, he wanted me to do accelerated math, which interested me but not as much as martial arts. He paid for my lessons finally and then ended up buying the dojo. We bought about ten of them after that, which I ran while I was in high school. I was...pretty single-minded.

"I joined the military after college where I got a degree in computer science, and turned the chain of dojos over to a good friend. The chain is doing really well, and always has. When we started training in hand-to-hand combat in boot camp, I knew what I was doing. Same with firearms. I was in Special Forces for eight years, doing things I can't talk about unless you have clearance for it. When I got out, I set up a company of my own as a security consultant. We're the people you call when you have a problem that can't land in the newspapers."

"The company must be doing very well," Harper said. "Private limo, the Ritz."

"Yeah." His company was one of the biggest in the world in that business.

The satellite phone vibrated soundlessly. Mark put the

earbud in and tapped it twice. "Yeah, talk to me."

Mike's voice was calm. "Thank God you were able to get a shot of the leader before he put the ski mask on. He's been identified as Pierre Hamidou, third-generation Algerian. Mentally unstable. He joined the police force in 2013 but proved too unstable and he was forced out. But evidently, he recruited some men. Four of the men are either current police officers or were in the police force. Bad business."

"Yeah." Mark thought through the consequences. "We don't know how high up this goes. Tell our contact at the DGSE not to share with any of the police authorities."

"Hard. But agreed."

"Mike..." Mark hesitated. This was unusual. He never hesitated when he spoke. But this was important.

Silence. Mike was waiting.

"I'm with a civilian here. She must be kept safe. I don't want her caught in the cross fire."

This was the first time—whether in the military or in his eight years running his company—that he'd had any consideration beyond the mission. Whatever Mike thought, Mark was deadly serious. He was not doing anything to endanger Harper.

"Roger that," Mike said.

"Your word."

"My word."

That was good enough for Mark.

"So. Is there a plan?"

"We're still working on one."

"Because I have one."

"I'm not surprised. Talk."

"The Dubrovka Theater scenario. Modified so it doesn't kill hostages."

Silence.

"And I need to be armed. I could grab one of the attackers and get his weapon but the leader, this Pierre Hamidou, keeps

checking in with his men. I could make it look like an acci-
dental death but nothing would explain away a lost weapon.
They'd tear down the building looking for it and someone
sooner or later will think of the hollow walls, which is where
we're holed up right now."

"I'll talk with our guy at the DGSE," Mike said. "He'll be in
touch soon."

"Roger that," Mark said and disconnected.

"The Dubrovka Theater scenario?" Harper asked.

Harper was smart but she was a civilian. She was nearly
overwhelmed as it was—trapped behind walls, with murderous
terrorists just feet away. A thousand ways to die. Mark didn't
want to flood her with data on something that might not be
viable. He hugged her closer, putting his mouth close to her ear
again.

"One of many possible scenarios," he said. "We'll have to
wait and see. And—" He stopped, looking at his cellphone
screen.

In the room outside, the two laptops came to life. CNN and
FRANCE1, both.

The sound was adjustable. Mark used the screen to direct
the tiny microphone toward the laptop showing CNN. He didn't
want the distraction of French.

BREAKING NEWS was on the red chyron scrolling across
the bottom. THE LOUVRE UNDER ATTACK.

The opening words of the anchorwoman were lost. Mark
finely adjusted the tiny directional mic. Suddenly, the anchorwoman's voice was as clear as if she were speaking next to him,
the FRANCE1 anchorman's voice a dull background noise.

The red chyron below the FRANCE1 anchorman read:
DERNIERE MINUTE: ATTAQUE TERRORISTE A LA
LOUVRE.

CNN. "For those just now tuning in, there is a developing
hostage crisis at the Louvre, in Paris, France. This morning at

10:35, there were shots at the entrance to the world-famous museum, under the Pyramid. The shots were closely followed by the sound of explosives as the entrance was blown up and buried under glass and stone. The famous Pyramid in the courtyard of the Louvre is no more."

On the screen appeared a helicopter shot of the internal courtyard of the Louvre with a jagged hole in the center. Mark heard Harper's sharp intake of breath as she realized what it was—the place the graceful glass Pyramid used to be. Her fingers dug into his thigh and he tightened his arm around her.

"As you can see, the Pyramid of the Louvre has been destroyed. Attackers swarmed through the famous museum and there are reports of many casualties. Exactly how many is unknown since the security cameras inside the museum have been turned off. We do have footage of the start of the attack from visitor cellphones. Some sent the footage to the police authorities. We are showing a selection of them. Warning— some of the footage is very graphic. Parents, be advised."

What followed was a gruesome montage with a soundtrack of screaming, terrified tourists. Running full out were men dressed in black with black balaclavas, shooting as they ran. Tourists falling. Some of the men were dressed in police uniforms.

People falling on the grand staircase, blood on the white stone, the images shaky, the sounds heartbreaking.

An apocalypse.

Harper watched wide-eyed, face pale, tears tracking down her face.

Even Mark, a battle-hardened soldier who'd seen plenty of blood spilled, felt his heart clench. These were civilians, innocent tourists. Men, women and children falling. Someone had had the time and decency to pixelate the faces of the children, but that did nothing to soften the blow of seeing their small bodies crumpled on the ground.

CNN cut back to the grim-faced anchor. "As you can see," she said, "it's a massacre. That is the only footage we have from inside the museum because at 11:10 a.m. all communications from cellphones inside the Louvre ceased. It is assumed that the terrorists effected a cellphone-coverage blackout."

She kept her voice even but her hands were gripping the sheets of paper on her desk.

"Here are some tourists who escaped from the terrible attack."

The screen cut to eyewitness accounts from shaken tourists. None of them came from the Gallery.

"The terrorists are now in the Salle des Etats, the room in the Louvre with eight world-famous paintings, including the *Mona Lisa*. And now—" She stopped, head down, hand pressed against her ear. She looked up into the camera. "Now for breaking news, we go to the CNN correspondent in Paris, Lyle Parsons, at the Élysée Palace. We have just been told that the president of the French Republic is going to be speaking."

The monitor switched to a scene in a great ceremonial room, huge chandeliers mirrored along the ornate walls.

Under the screen was another chyron. *Hervé de Montigny, President of France, addresses the nation.*

The president began talking and Mark followed the subtitles.

"Today all of France is under attack. An attack on the Louvre is an attack on the heart of all French women and men. It is an attack on the world. There are dead men and women lying in the halls of the very symbol of French civilization, and a number of people are being held hostage in the Salle des Etats, under the *Mona Lisa*, which was attacked as well."

The video shifted to the shot of Pierre Hamidou looking like he was going to behead the blonde tourist, instead swiveling and slashing the painting behind him.

The screen cut back to the president. "To the despicable

men now holding hostages in the Salle des Etats in the Louvre, we say this: we will never negotiate with barbarians, with terrorists."

The screen cut back to the studio, the anchorwoman looking somber. She'd clearly been briefed on the threats coming from the terrorists. "What the president didn't state was the requests of the terrorists. CNN has sources saying that the Louvre attackers wish to swap the hostages for terrorists being held by French law enforcement. To understand the situation better, we have terrorism expert Manuel LaVarga in our studio. Mr. LaVarga, how would you describe the current situation in the Louvre?"

Mark studied LaVarga's face carefully. He'd had dealings with LaVarga before and found him to be tough and smart.

"Well, I'd say right now that this is a classic stalemate. The attackers have managed to fortify themselves in the middle of a huge building where they would have ample notice if French soldiers were to attack. Word is that they have planted explosives, and besides wanting to keep the hostages safe, I can say that there isn't a Frenchman alive whose heart doesn't quake at the thought of the destruction of the Louvre. And there isn't a Frenchman alive who isn't heartbroken at the destruction of the Pyramid.

"So the attackers—and we don't know their affiliation as of this moment, whether they are ISIS or Al-Qaeda or any of their offshoots—are in a way protected by hundreds of thousands of square feet of building that law enforcement and the military do not wish to see harmed. They are holding over a hundred hostages and will no doubt start killing them if their demands are not met. And you have just heard the French president say that France does not negotiate with terrorists. So—stalemate."

"Is that French policy? Not negotiating with terrorists?"

LaVarga nodded. "It is. The French over the course of the past decade have taken a hard line on terrorism, having suffered numerous attacks on their citizenry. The French president means it. No negotiation. But that doesn't leave the authorities many cards to play."

"Thank you for that analysis, Manuel." The anchor swiveled a little in her chair and faced forward. "That about wraps up what we know at this time. Over one hundred hostages are being held in the Louvre by terrorists who shot their way in, leaving behind hundreds of dead bodies. At this moment, we have no idea exactly how many victims are lying dead in the halls of the museum. The terrorists have defaced the most important painting in the world, the *Mona Lisa*. They have blown up the famous entrance to the museum, the glass Pyramid. They threaten to kill the hostages and blow up the world-famous museum if their demands to free what they call political prisoners are not met. Stay tuned for further news on the ongoing hostage crisis at the Louvre."

The FRANCE1 anchorman was still talking. Mark slipped his earbud to Harper and positioned the mini mike so that it was picking up the French channel clearly.

His satphone vibrated. Mike. "What do you have for me?"

"The head of Action Division of the DGSE on the line."

Mark wanted to know one thing. "Do you trust him? Him personally?"

"Yes," Mike answered, "I do. Absolutely."

That was enough for Mark. Mark's expertise was the Middle East and Mike's was Europe. "Can you patch me through?"

"Roger that. Hold." There were a series of clicks and whistles, most of which were encryption and decryption. They were being routed from satellite to satellite and station to station. "Okay, Mark, you're a go. You're speaking with the director of Action Division, Serge Robert." Mike pronounced it Roh-*ber*.

"Mr. Redmond." A deep voice with a faint accent came online.

Harper must have realized that something was going on. She'd been listening carefully, taking notes in a little booklet of notepaper, but now she looked up at him, a question in her eyes.

He kissed her gently on the forehead and rotated his finger. *Tell you later.*

She nodded and went back to listening to French TV.

"Mr. Robert," Mark answered. He had a ton of respect for the DGSE. They were tough and smart and hard-asses, every one. "You understand the situation."

"I do," the deep voice answered. "And I've seen the video."

"I'm going to send all my videos, if you give me your number."

"Excellent."

Robert gave his number and Mark sent him everything his cellphone had recorded. It would be a lot more intel than the propaganda video broadcast. It would give the number of terrorists in the room, weaponry, position with regard to the hostages. Not to mention the uncovered faces.

"Received. Excellent intel. I understand you're in a concealed position," Robert said.

"We're in a concealed position." Mark met Harper's eyes. "There are two of us, myself and a woman. Her safety is paramount." Mark was willing to go on the attack if they could arm him but only if he could mount that attack far away from Harper.

"Understood," Robert murmured. "Can you state your position?"

"We are inside the walls of the *Mona Lisa* room. The walls have an internal space. We're fairly well concealed, but the entrance to most of the side rooms of the Grand Gallery are covered by armed men."

"Understood. We're working on a plan. We are also considering your proposal of the Moscow Dubrovka Theater scenario."

Good. So far it was the only way out that Mark could see. Except for the fact that in Moscow, people died at the hands of the police rescuing them. And in this case, the police could also be part of the problem.

"Do you understand why I had Mike contact you and not the police?"

"I do." Robert's voice turned grim. "Excellent call. Not only is the ringleader a former police officer—though for only a few months—but we've identified three of the men in the video you sent me. The intel just came in. They are all in some way connected to the police force. Two were briefly agents, one applied but didn't make the grade. I'm sending you their police ID photos and the job application photo of the one who didn't make it into the police."

On Mark's screen were mug shots of young police recruits. They were clean shaven and the men on the other side of the wall all had beards, but he could see the matchups.

"It means they'll have some tactical skills."

"Not as good as ours," Robert vowed.

Yes, the agents of the DGSE were notoriously capable and well trained. They had a rep as fierce and effective and if they had to overstep some laws to get their guy, so be it.

"Sir," Mark said. "I'm here. Use me. Just make sure my companion is kept safe."

"Roger that, Mr. Redmond. Make sure we know if and when you move."

"I'll expect to hear from you soon."

Mark disconnected and put both arms around Harper. She was shivering though it was warm inside the walls. One way to help her was to keep her busy.

"What did they say on the French TV channel?"

She licked dry lips and Mark handed over a small water

bottle. There was no way of knowing how long they'd be trapped here but for now, he wouldn't stop her drinking her fill. He could do without. But she just sipped and handed him back the bottle.

He refused to take the bottle. "Drink more."

Harper shook her head. "I don't want to finish our water supply too soon. We don't know how long we'll be here."

That was true but Mark didn't think the siege would last days like the Beslan or Moscow theater sieges. It was too big a thing. Public opinion would be like a tsunami bearing down on the Interior Ministry's walls.

"Plus," Harper looked up with a small smile, holding out the bottle to him again, "you need to drink some water, too."

Something squeezed inside his chest. Terrified and shocked, having witnessed something that nauseated a battle-hardened warrior, she still thought of him. He gently pushed the bottle back to her.

"Don't worry about me." Mark ran the back of his forefinger down her cheek, marveling again at the softness of her skin. "I've been trained to go without water longer than most people can stand."

"And have you?" she asked, her voice barely above a whisper. Her eyes in the dim light glowed silver.

He nodded. Oh yeah. Yeah, he had. Three and a half days was his limit, when he started showing strong signs of severe dehydration. Headache, dizziness, orthostatic hypotension. When immediate hydration became necessary, at the risk of permanent organ damage.

That was when he knew he had to break cover and seek water. He'd done it and survived.

She tapped the water bottle against his chest, hard. "We're going to share this bottle, and even that is unfair. You're twice my size, you should be getting at least two thirds of the water."

He smiled at her. She didn't smile back and tapped the bottom of the bottle insistently against his chest again.

"You're serious," Mark said, surprised.

"Damn right I am." She held the half-empty bottle up and he took it. "I want to see you finish it."

"I only have four bottles." Mark shook his head.

"That's four bottles more than I have. I didn't even think to bring water with me. It's thanks to your foresight that we have water at all. And," her mouth tightened, "something tells me that this will come to a head soon. I don't see the French allowing a prolonged siege."

She was right. Mark upended the bottle and finished it. He felt instantly refreshed. She'd been right about that, too.

Something else tapped against his hand and he looked down in surprise at the protein bar. Half of one, anyway, which she was holding out to him.

He batted her hand away but it returned back to his mouth like iron to a magnet.

She narrowed her eyes as him. "We're sharing this, too. And don't argue."

She sounded for a second like his first drill instructor. Like the Voice of God, only a whispering soprano instead of a bellowing basso profundo. A voice you never, ever disobeyed.

"Yes, ma'am." He took it and they both finished their halves quickly.

Harper reached out and cupped his chin. "I don't want you suffering because of me."

This was all wrong. *He* was the warrior, the protector. No one ever worried about him.

Mark moved her hand up over his chin to cover his mouth and kissed the palm of her hand. There was something about this—the extreme danger on the other side of the wall, twelve armed murderers ready to kill at a moment's notice, and tenderness on the inside of that wall—that touched him deeply.

In danger, he always switched straight into battle mode. A way of being that allowed him to think and react to danger without any emotions getting in the way. He'd always gone into battle having made peace with the idea that he might not survive. All warriors did. You couldn't feel in battle. Feelings were dangerous, toxic even.

And here he was, swamped with them. Pierced by feelings thumping around in his chest, all of them having to do with the beautiful woman sitting hip to hip beside him.

He kissed her hand again, held it.

"I'm not suffering." Truer words were never spoken. Even with the imminent danger they were in, there wasn't anyplace in the world he wanted to be other than right here, right beside Harper Kendall.

"Good," she said. Her hand curled tightly around his own, eyes locked on his.

"Tell me what they said on French TV."

"Okay." She caught a deep breath, let it out slowly. "The French channel essentially just kept repeating what we know. The Pyramid was blown up, an unknown number of terrorists swarmed the Denon Wing, which is where we are, explosives were set along the monumental staircase and at the entrance to the Grand Gallery. Nobody knows how many bodies are lying along the corridors, but 6,504 tickets were sold for today and by the time the attack started, 4,752 people had entered the museum. Many people escaped before the police arrived, but nobody knows exactly how many. Estimates of the dead range from the hundreds to the thousands."

Privately, Mark thought it was closer to thousands of dead rather than hundreds. The terrorists had moved fast and they had automatic rifles. He was certain that it was a true slaughterhouse out there, particularly at the entrance. And it could become a slaughterhouse in the *Mona Lisa* room, too. He would do everything in his power to stop that.

"The news program interviewed the mayor of Paris, the head of the Louvre and the head of the police force."

Mark huffed out his breath in disgust. "Who presumably didn't mention that a number of the attackers are former cops. And that some of them were in police uniform." It wasn't a question.

"No." Harper stared at her knees and sighed. "They didn't add anything of substance, either. Shock that this has happened, convinced that the forces of law and order will prevail, the country will stand firm... Rhetoric, really."

She shook her head, shiny hair slipping over her shoulder. Every time she moved he could smell her perfume and shampoo, delicate fragrances that brought life and beauty into this dusty wall.

Even covered in dust and scared to death, she was still so beautiful. Part of it was pure genetic luck, part of it that bone-deep classiness, refined and discerning. Not a woman designed for the field.

He'd been the tip of the spear so many times. Out in the field, life was raw, crude. When he came back from the bloodiest missions, it took him a couple of days to shake the chaos and ugliness of the world from his soul.

This was the first time he was near terrorists with a woman he cared for and it shook something deep inside him. It wasn't right that she should be here—a wall away from murderers, blood-crazed thugs one step up from animals. It upset him at a deep level. She belonged far away from this. She belonged somewhere safe, writing books and thinking about design. Doing things that could be done only because the peace was kept by warriors. This wasn't her place at all.

But here she was.

Mark lifted her chin. Her eyes rose to his. The narrow,

intense flashlight beam lit her face up from below, caressing the elegant bones. He bent to kiss her, intending a short, reassuring kiss.

But there, in that small, dark space, with murderers right on the other side of the wall, desire rose—swift, sharp, unbelievably intense. A force he was unable to resist. If he was holding her in his arms, she was safe. While he was alive and close enough to touch her, she'd be safe.

And kissing her felt like an antidote to all that was on the other side of that wall. Her mouth tasted delicious, she smelled like flowers in warm sunshine, she felt as soft as silk.

Harper was clutching his shoulders, shaking. She was scared. He tightened his arms around her, meaning it to be reassuring, like a hug. But it didn't reassure him, it aroused him. Her breasts flattened against his chest and he remembered what those breasts felt like naked. Her skin had been hot, her scent rising from it like a cloud last night.

Last night they'd both been wide open. The world had faded to a dream beyond the hotel walls. Anything he could have wished for and desired had been right in that room, in his arms.

But now danger loomed beyond the stucco walls, monsters right outside, willing and able to hurt them, kill them. They had killed maybe a thousand tourists already and were threatening to massacre over a hundred more.

But crazily enough, that wasn't important while he kissed her. The danger beyond the walls inflamed him, was like a spear at his back, spurring him on.

He left her mouth to nibble along her jawline and felt more than heard her sigh. That narrow rib cage lifting and falling as her long neck lay open to him. He ran his lips and then his tongue along the tendon of her neck, feeling her shudder, then brought his mouth back up to her jaw, behind her ear.

Her scent was concentrated there, in the hollow behind her

ear, her hair forming a perfumed curtain that cut off the world even more.

Mark nipped her, gently and carefully, but with enough force to make her jerk and gasp. Exactly the way a stallion nips his mare, to make her hold still, to make her remember who she belongs to.

She belonged to him.

He'd found her, he was going to keep her.

Their heads aligned and now they were kissing deeply, wildly. Harper's arms locked behind his neck and she pulled as if wanting him as close to her as possible. Fine, because he wanted the same thing.

Closeness. Skin to skin. Touching that smooth fragrant softness all over. Closer, *closer*, because everything good in the world was right there, right with her, right *in* her.

Mark shifted, put his hand behind her head to cushion it and shifted them down inside the small corridor, him atop her. One hand still cupping her head, he pulled off the short wool jacket then pulled her silk sweater up and off, unhooking her bra, lifting his head up just enough to see her.

She was so beautiful she nearly blinded him. The flashlight *was* blinding him, so he shifted it slightly so it wasn't right in his eyes.

God. Just look at her, he thought.

The bright beam of the flashlight picked out the bright highlights of her hair that surrounded her head like a halo. She was staring up at him, eyes glowing almost silver, half closed with desire. Her mouth was red, swollen from his kisses, branded by him. There was a tiny mark under her ear made by his mouth. All that smooth skin, those small, perfect, upright breasts with the pale pink nipples...he wanted to just gobble her up.

Though he wanted to kiss her mouth again, kiss her until they both passed out from lack of air, he wanted to kiss her breasts even more. He remembered their taste, like salty vanilla; he remembered her nipples hardening against his tongue; he remembered sucking strongly, hearing her deep panting in time with the pulls of his mouth.

Oh yeah.

He wanted that again, he wanted that *right now*.

Mark dipped his head, kissed his way from her chin, down over her neck, to her breasts. Harper was amazingly responsive and he was paying close attention. Real close attention. She was like a map where the waystations moaned. She let him know clearly what pleased her. Everything pleased her but some things pleased her *more*.

The space under her ear, for example. All he had to do was suck a little there and she'd arch her neck. A little nip right where her neck met her shoulder and she'd jolt. And when he licked her nipples and blew on them, she'd catch her breath and forget to breath out. He'd have to go to her mouth and kiss her briefly so she'd breathe again.

How could a woman be so perfect?

The light here was both dim and harsh. Military flashlights weren't built to caress skin, but it did hers. Her skin actually glowed, like pearls in the dark. And there was enough light to see where she changed color. Like her nipples, turning bright pink. Like the flush that covered her from her face to her breasts when she came.

Fuck, he had to see that color again, there was nothing like it. When Harper came, it was a feast for every sense—the colors, feeling her muscles tighten, that burst of scent that came from her skin and her sex.

The confines of the space between the walls and the imperative need to stay silent made it somehow more exciting. In some dim part of Mark's normally disciplined brain he realized this was madness—sex while terrorists with guns stood mere feet away from them was insane. But he couldn't have stopped, not for anything in the world, not even with a gun to his head.

He had to be inside Harper. Or die.

But first...

Mark licked one nipple, then sucked, hard. Her left breast trembled from her fast-beating heart. He could see it and he could feel it.

He slipped her panties off, this delightful little silky lace thing, sliding it right down her legs, tossing it to the side. Now she was naked except for her skirt, which somehow made the whole thing even sexier. He couldn't see her sex but he could feel it. He cupped her between her legs, waggling his hand a little to make her open her legs wider. She obeyed instantly, her heels sliding along the dusty floor making a little scraping sound.

Mark ran his finger around her sex. He had rough skin on his hands and hoped he wasn't hurting her. He lifted his mouth from her breast to look at her. She didn't look like she was hurting. Her eyes were half-closed, light gray eyes looking like slices of a dawn sky. She was breathing heavily, that narrow rib cage rising and falling fast, nipples hard and cherry red, one glistening from his mouth.

"Mark," she whispered, and lifted her hand to the back of his head and pressed. It was a command, and he obeyed happily, bending back to her breast. When he pulled at her nipple, she sighed and arched her back.

She was already wet, ready. He wanted her even more ready and slipped his finger inside her. Harper's breath left her in a whoosh and he abandoned her breast because he wanted to watch her face. He slid his finger in, then out, watching her carefully. She let him know where she loved to be touched, without words. They didn't need words. He just watched her beautiful face, watched the color rise, her eyes flutter, her mouth open to take in more air.

His hand speeded up, moving in her faster and faster, and when his thumb touched her, right *there*, she shuddered, took in a breath, and he pulled his free hand from the back of her head and clamped it over her mouth as she came, feeling her convulse around his finger, while also feeling her panting against the palm of his hand.

At the last second, she realized she shouldn't be making any noise, but a few raw groans escaped as her orgasm rippled through her.

His turn.

All he had to do was unzip, slide his briefs down and move on top of her. Mark slid a second finger inside her, opening her up, and slid into her, not bothering to go slowly. He didn't have the control to enter her slowly. He planted his hands on either side of her head and pumped into her, fast and hard, his mouth covering hers. She was still coming as he moved in her, her hands clutching his shoulders, ankles locked over his buttocks, riding him.

It was too intense to last. A streak of electric heat ran down his backbone, through his balls, out his dick, which swelled and exploded. He came and came and came, spurting every drop of liquid in his body as he shuddered and shook inside her, completely out of control. Static filled his head, wiping out any thoughts that may have been there.

He stilled, closed his eyes, dropped his forehead to her shoulder. Harper's ankles unlocked at the small of his back and her legs fell to the sides. Her arms, too, slid down as if she didn't have the strength to hold him for even a second longer.

Mark waited for his heartbeat to slow down, for his breathing to even out, for the slight tremors running through his body to still.

It took a while. But finally, after a billion years, he sprawled over her, wiped out.

8

Harper wriggled a little, just enough to slightly angle her torso out from under his. Just enough to breathe a little. She didn't want him off her, she just wanted a little oxygen. Just a bit.

Because though he was heavy as an ox, he felt absolutely delicious. Hard as a rock all over, except the bit that had been inside her and was now softening, starting to slip out of her.

God, it had been glorious. Almost better than last night, and last night had been off the charts.

And it has also been...insane.

Passion had never, ever gotten the best of her. Except now, apparently. There had been nothing in her head except red-hot heat, a crazy desire to have Mark Redmond on her, in her. And nothing was going to stand in her way. Certainly not a dozen murderous terrorists a few feet away, separated from her by some wood and stucco.

God.

What had she been thinking?

She hadn't. She hadn't been thinking, at all.

But she *had* been feeling, emotions raw and harsh, right

under her skin. The horror of having watched people being killed—gunned down like animals. Men standing with weapons trained on terrified hostages, sitting on the floor like animals ready for slaughter. Women and children, not knowing if they would get out alive.

The Louvre was wired for destruction. That was one scenario where she and Mark would not survive. They'd wired the monumental staircase and the Grand Gallery, so explosives were not far away. They'd die in the initial blast or be buried under tons of stone.

Given that, making love with Mark—perhaps the last act of their lives—made perfect sense. They'd be crazy not to.

She was nearly naked. Jacket, sweater, bra off, panties thrown somewhere. Her only item of clothing was her skirt twisted around her waist.

Mark, on the other hand, was still sort of halfway decent. He even had his windbreaker still on. He'd just opened his pants and pushed his briefs down. In a second, he'd look normal. The only place he was naked was where he was still connected to her.

But holding him still felt really good. Harper could feel his hard muscles through the layers of cloth. She tightened her arms around him, holding on as close as she could to all that power and strength, as if it could pass through him into her, then dropped her arms and legs to the dusty floor because she had no strength at all left.

Turning her head, she sniffed at his neck, lips curling in a helpless smile as she kissed him. He hardened inside her in response, but she shook her head. No way could she have another round. Her muscles were reduced to jelly.

He smelled good, too, though she could also smell the funk of sweat and, embarrassingly, she could also smell the sex coming from their groins. His juices and hers.

His juices...

God.

They hadn't used a condom! It hadn't even occurred to her to think of birth control. The desire had been too elemental, too fierce, to think of anything but having him inside her. To have an orgasm that nearly blew her head apart.

"Mark!" she whispered fiercely in his ear. "We didn't use—"

"A condom," he sighed as he pulled out of her and lifted himself on his forearms. His face was right above hers and he looked her straight in the eyes. "I have to confess I didn't think of it. Didn't even cross my mind."

"Mine, either." It had to be said. She'd been as mindless as he had. "I'm always so very careful."

"Me, too." He bent briefly, kissed the tip of her nose. "But I have regular checkups and like I said, I'm always careful. Or was, until this moment. I'm clean, though. Guaranteed."

She nodded. *Me, too.*

But of course, *no condom* was more than just an issue of possible disease.

"What if—"

"Shh." He kissed the side of her mouth this time. "It'll be all right. Whatever happens, I'm with you. I'm not going anywhere. We're in this together."

And those words, just like that, changed something inside her. He was still the insanely attractive, super-macho male who'd intrigued her. That hadn't changed. What changed was in her. His face, right above hers, had morphed. It wasn't simply an attractive stranger's face. No, it had become the face of someone who'd carved a place in her heart. Crazy as it sounded, he was part of her.

There was an almost magnetic component to their bodies, they almost clicked when they touched each other, as if they'd have to be pulled apart. The French had a saying for people who'd bonded. *Les atomes crochues.* Their very atoms had intertwined.

Even crazier, she felt like she was looking at her future.

Alarming. Exhilarating. Both, at the same time. Particularly since they might not have a future at all.

"Come." Mark stood, pulled his pants and briefs over his hips and zipped up. Just like that, in a matter of seconds, he was back to normal. She, on the other hand, looked like a wanton woman, lying on her back, naked except for the soft skirt wrapped around her waist.

Mark held out a huge hand and easily lifted her to her feet. She should have felt ashamed or at least awkward, but she didn't. They'd shared a moment of intense closeness and next to that, it didn't make any difference that she was standing there half naked, her clothes scattered on the floor.

Mark stepped forward and put his arms around her. Her own arms automatically went around his waist and she once again felt all that power flowing into her. He kissed the top of her head, bent his mouth to her ear.

"I'm not sorry."

She gave a sharp shake of her head against his shoulder. "No." There was a whirlwind of emotions in her—sharp and raw—but regret wasn't one of them.

He pulled away slightly. "Here, honey. Let me help you."

Harper stood like a doll while he picked up her bra from the floor, holding out her arms obediently as he put it on her and fastened it in back.

"Up," he said softly, and her hands shot up so he could slide the silk sweater down her arms. He pulled the hem down over her waist, smoothed the fabric over her hips. His eyes followed his hands and in the harsh light of the flashlight, the edges of his face grew harder.

He bent to pick up her panties and held them for a long moment. The pale cream lace looked amazingly sexy in his big, rough hands, a study in contrasts.

Mark knelt to help her put her panties back on, but then

once on his knees, he stilled. He glanced up at her once, then fixated on her mound, eyes unwavering.

Looking down, Harper saw his dark, short hair, stubby eyelashes, straight nose, sharp cheekbones, all foreshortened, like in some Renaissance painting showing perspective. She couldn't quite see his expression, but she knew what it was. God knew she'd seen it often enough lately. He was aroused. It was clear in the ruddy cheeks, tight skin over his temples, harsh breathing.

How could he possibly be aroused? They'd just had incredibly intense and exhausting sex. How could he want more? How could—

Mark leaned forward, eyes narrowed. His thumbs opened her and he ran his tongue along her sex, and her legs trembled.

Oh. That's how. If you'd asked her, she'd have said that she couldn't have any kind of sex, she was just tapped out. But apparently her body—which she was starting to realize she didn't know as well as she thought she did—had reserves. Who knew?

Mark opened his mouth and kissed her there, exactly as if it were her mouth. Licking and nibbling and taking little bites. It was so intense she couldn't stand. She needed to sit down or lie down. Or something.

But somehow his hands were holding her up, he wouldn't let her fall while he was devouring her alive.

Mark stopped, looked up at her. Though the light was dim, she could see that he was flushed, lips colored dark red, eyes deep and luminous.

"I can smell us—you and me. I can taste both of us."

Her knees wobbled. The idea, the image, of her body containing her juices and his semen—crazily, it turned her on. Usually she rushed to the shower to wash the smell of sex off her but this time she didn't want that. They'd had raw sex and it was right that she still smelled and tasted of him. She tried to say that but nothing came from her throat but air.

Mark's mouth and tongue were hot on already inflamed tissues. It was way too intense and she tried to evade his mouth but those big, strong hands held her fast, there was no escape, nothing to do but endure. Everything inside her seemed to curl inward, spiraling tighter and tighter until she had to close her eyes and stop breathing, and still everything became more intense, spiraling more and more...

The wave crested and broke and Harper drew in a deep breath but before she could moan, his big hand covered her mouth and she ended up making a muffled keening sound into his palm. She was sweating and shaking, prickly heat sliding under her skin, her hands clutching his head, the one steady thing in a roiling ocean of sheer pleasure.

Harper's legs were weak and shaking and could barely hold her up. Mark waited for her to find her balance, then lifted one foot then the other foot into her panties and slowly pulled the stretchy lace up her legs. He held her hips, the soft skirt falling over his hands as he rose to his full height.

Harper watched him rise helplessly. He was somehow dominating her body without bending her will to him. Her body followed his blindly. She was helplessly plugged in to what he wanted because she wanted it too. If you'd asked her if she wanted another round of sex, she'd have said no. Hell no, even. Until he had pressed his face against her belly and then that crazy switch inside her flipped to *whatever Mark wants* mode.

When he removed his hands from her hips, the skirt fell to mid-calf and, like Mark, she was decent again.

He cupped her face, his hands entirely covering the sides of her head, and bent forward until his forehead touched hers.

"What are you doing to me?" he asked.

That was rich. What was *she* doing to *him?* Harper gave a weak laugh. "You're kidding, right?"

Mark shook his head. "I've lost control. I never lose control."

"Me either." It was true. Harper prided herself on her self-control, on not being swayed by anything or anyone.

The only good thing about this was that she wasn't alone. He was just like her—both caught in a wild river flowing downhill, smashing into boulders and logs, unable to control their movements.

"You shouldn't be so beautiful and fascinating," he complained. "It's not fair."

At that, Harper smiled. "So..." She waved a forefinger between them, tapping her chest, tapping his. "This. This is all my fault?"

He sighed. "God yeah. I'm helpless to resist you."

Suddenly the reality of their situation came crashing in on her. "That's so dangerous," she whispered. "We're not at the Ritz."

Mark blew out a breath and stood straight, putting a few inches between them. "No, we're not. I'm not sorry I couldn't resist you, but we need to put that behind us now." He stared down into her eyes, curling a lock of her hair behind her ear. "Until we can get back to the Ritz."

Tears welled suddenly in her eyes and she had to blink hard to keep them from spilling over. The Ritz. How she missed it! Not the luxury so much as the feeling of civility and normality it represented. If terrorists blew up the Louvre, it would be as bad as 9/11. Another spate of wars would ensue. Their world would be changed forever.

"I can't wait to get back to the Ritz."

"That's my girl. Focus on that. We'll get through this."

"Will we?" And this time tears spilled over. Mortified, she swiped at her cheeks. "Oh, God, I'm so sorry!"

The last thing she wanted was to be a dead weight to Mark,

a sniveler, someone he had to worry about in these dangerous circumstances.

"That's okay. I get it that you're scared. I'm scared, too."

She looked at him, tall and broad and so strong it was almost absurd. "Yeah, right."

"No, really. The only difference is that I've been trained to deal with it." Mark looked her over, more like a comrade checking for wounds than a lover. "Okay. Let's see what we have here."

He did something to that cellphone so that it continued showing the *Mona Lisa* room without the cable connection. The image lost a tiny bit of clarity as he took her hand and walked them farther into the walls until they were in the back of an adjoining room. He made her sit down with her back to the wall, cross-legged, then sat down himself, long legs bent. He reached into his backpack and handed her a fresh bottle of water. Two down, two to go.

She cracked the top, drank half, handed him the bottle. Gave him a steely look until he finished it.

"So—you're scared?" she asked him.

"I'd be crazy not to be scared. Anything can happen and there's a lot of weaponry out there. But I learned a long time ago to channel fear and master it. It's there but it's controllable. We're not dying. Not today."

The way he said it, not boasting, just stating a fact, was actually reassuring.

"That guy you were talking to. The head of the DGSE."

"Robert?"

"Yeah. You were talking about the Dubrovka Theater scenario. What's that?"

Mark stared as his knees for a moment, then sighed. "On the 23rd of October, 2002, forty Chechen terrorists overran a theater in Moscow that was showing a very popular musical. There were over 850 members of the audience surrounded by terrorists who were demanding the end of the Second Chechen War."

"About as likely as our terrorists demanding the release of prisoners," she said dryly.

"Yeah. They kept the hostages without food and water for almost three days and had started murdering them—two women were shot and killed. Russian Special Forces couldn't storm the place because they'd have had to rush down about a hundred feet of corridor manned by terrorists and then up a staircase before reaching the theater itself. And the terrorists had set explosives all around, and heavy explosives in the middle of the hostages."

She pulled in a shocked breath. She could see it—a replica of what was on the other side of the wall. A long corridor before reaching the hostages, explosives set along the way...

"Like here."

"Like here." Mark nodded. "No way to get to the terrorists without unacceptable casualties, and in the time it would take to get to the terrorists, they could wipe out the hostages. An impossible situation."

"What did they do?"

"They gassed the place."

Her voice was a shocked whisper. "They *what*?"

"They gassed the place. They never announced what they used but everyone agrees it was an opiate, a strong one. Probably Fentanyl."

"The one that's causing so many deaths in the opioid crisis?"

His mouth tightened. "That's the one. It's a thousand times more effective than opium. Very fast acting. But very dangerous. Out of the almost 900 hostages, about 170 died from the drug."

"Conquering the disease but killing the patient."

"That's right. But I'm trusting that Robert has something

better. As powerful and as fast-acting but that won't kill the hostages. Or that they will come with a drug that can counter the effects fast."

Harper thought about it.

"Could they send the drug through the ventilation system?"

Mark glanced at her. "Smart thinking, but no, they can't. They shut off all electricity in the Louvre, all systems are down. The lighting they have is via generators they brought up. So I think Robert's best solution would be to somehow get something to me that I can pump into the room. From what I understand, that is the only room where they have live hostages." He waited a beat, took her hand in his. His voice turned gentle. "Honey, I think we're going to have to assume that any tourists they have in the halls or in the building are dead. It takes a hell of a lot of manpower to keep living hostages prisoners. I'm assuming that the only ones left alive are in the *Mona Lisa* room."

Harper stared at her knees, thinking of how many dead there must be out there. But not all of those innocent people were dead. There was still a room full of people they might be able to save. She had to help Mark in any way she could, trying to recall schematics she'd once seen in an archive of architectural drawings.

She elbowed him. "Mark, there are chimney pots at regular intervals along the Louvre roofline. It would be dangerous because it's a mansard roof and slopes very steeply. But if they can lower everything we need through the chimney pots to this level, we could do it."

She could see the whites of his eyes. "We? What do you mean *we*?"

"You need me. I know the Louvre. This morning at the entrance, I wasn't paying any attention, but I'm paying attention now. If we need to emerge from the walls, I know how to get to where we have to go as quickly as possible."

"No." Mark shook his head. "I studied the map. I'm not having you emerging from these walls. Absolutely not."

"Mark." She touched his arm and felt his muscles almost vibrating with tension. "What you studied was a tourist's map that shows just the main rooms and corridors. It's not a complete map. I know I got a little turned around this morning, but I still know the place better than you possibly can. And you don't know what they're going to give you. I can help you carry things."

His jaw muscles worked. "You are going to stay right here, flat on the ground. If shooting starts, they will aim for head height. It's almost impossible for them to hit you if you're on the ground, the angles would be all wrong."

For a second, Harper was tempted. Really tempted. Let Mark do his thing. He was trained for this and—she had a master's in art history. Staying flat on the ground in a possible shooting scenario sounded like a very smart idea.

But—brave as he was, Mark was one person, operating in a building he'd never been in before.

All her life, Harper had loved art. Even as a little girl, her mother had bought her art books she'd pored over instead of toys. Everything about the Louvre was what she believed in from the bottom of her heart. Mankind was brutal, greedy, unforgiving. Men fomented wars, tortured and enslaved people.

Mankind also produced beautiful things, things that elevated the soul, made us more than brutes.

If she stayed cowering on the floor while Mark went out alone, what would the rest of her life be like?

A lie.

"I want to come with you. I must come with you," she said calmly. Her fingers clutched his arm. "I won't get in your way, I just want to help, and I think I can. If shooting starts—"

She swallowed. She'd never been near shooting but she'd

watched a lot of films. It didn't take much imagination to picture the two of them, broken and bleeding on the shiny parquet floor.

And she imagined waiting on the dusty floor between walls for Mark to come back. Waiting for the sounds of gunfire, waiting...

"If shooting starts," she continued, keeping her voice steady, "I'm not guaranteed safety, anyway. I'd rather be out. I'd rather be with you."

"No," he said through gritted teeth, his jaws so tense it was hard for him to get the word out of his mouth.

"I'd be safer with you."

"No." She could almost hear his teeth grinding.

"We're a team, Mark." She dealt what she thought would be the killing blow. "Last night made us a team. We do this together or we don't do it at all."

He blew out his breath and hung his head between his shoulders.

Harper said nothing, just watched him, hand on his clenched arm. There was nothing more she could say. What she'd said made sense. She knew the hidden byways of the Louvre, certainly better than he did. She could help carry equipment. And she believed from the bottom of her heart that she'd be safer by his side. There was just something about him —his physical grace, his quiet efficiency—that made her believe in him.

His head lifted. "You follow what I say. You jump when I say jump, you run when I say run. No questions asked."

Her heart leaped. It leaped in fear and hope. She was afraid of what they would have to do. But she wanted with every cell in her body to be near him. And a quivering, terrified but determined part of her wanted—fiercely—to help stop an atrocity.

"Yes, absolutely."

"You stay with me at all times unless I tell you otherwise."

"Count on it."

He turned and caught her up in a hug so strong it hurt. She didn't care. She hugged him right back.

"I don't want anything to happen to you." Crazily, she felt a shudder go through him. Through this big, hard, tough man.

"Neither do I," she said, and he gave a little huff of a laugh, dropping his head to her shoulder for a moment.

He pulled back and shook his head. "I don't like it, I don't—"

His satphone's screen lit up.

"Jesus. It's Robert." Mark was breathing heavily, as if he'd just run a ten-mile race. His looked at the screen and tapped his earbud. "Go."

Harper couldn't hear what was being said, heard only his part of the conversation and it was mainly *yes* and *understood*.

But one thing he made clear. "Let's do this now, tonight. And don't let the police know. We don't know if there's a mole. If there is, you'll lose the advantage of surprise and we'll lose our lives. And by 'we', remember that there's a person with me. A woman. If something happens to me, you find her and protect her with everything you've got, is that understood?"

Robert said something that made Mark grunt.

"Okay." He checked his watch. Reflexively, Harper checked her own. It was a little past 6 p.m. Last night, she'd checked her watch at 6 p.m., getting ready for dinner with Mark, glancing out the window. Darkness had begun falling over the City of Light. They couldn't see the outside world, but it was getting dark out there.

Mark nodded, a sharp movement of his head. "So it's a go for 3 a.m. Show me on a detailed map you text me where the drop will be. And we coordinate the attack. I'll let you know when everyone is sedated. Your troops will have naloxone, correct?"

Naloxone, she knew from having read a billion articles on the opioid crisis, counteracted opioid-based drugs.

It was amazing how he was able to keep his deep voice quiet. She barely heard him yet she was only inches away.

"Roger that. I also want comms, two sets, plus two sets of body armor, one for a very small person, two EH-20 gas masks or the equivalent, an MP5 with a belt of at least five magazines. A Glock 19, holster and ammo." He listened, nodded. "Keep this in DGSE, and don't let the police know. Your guys have to operate as a separate unit from the other LE forces. And dig deep into the police. If you look hard, you'll find your mole. Get either the NSA or GCHQ in the UK to monitor calls with AI, sifting through code words. When you find him or them, isolate them. If the terrorists get wind of what we're doing, it'll be a massacre. Over and out."

He tapped his earbud. Then he switched over to the cellphone screen and turned the phone so she could see, too.

It was dark in the room, the only illumination four spotlights in the four corners, lighting up the ceiling. Harper could barely make out the hostages huddled on the ground, darker shapes in the darkness. She could only imagine how horrible it must be, mothers trying to soothe their children while being terrified themselves. Men wondering how they could protect their families against armed terrorists. Not knowing if the end was near. Knowing they might die in the next minute.

The leader was in one corner, talking to two of his men. The others were patrolling, but not in an organized way. They seemed to simply walk back and forth along the walls. Two were still posted at the entrance. Harper studied them carefully. They twitched and moved from booted foot to booted foot. One beat a tattoo against his submachine gun nervously. The other bopped his head to some beat only he could hear.

"Are they *high*?" she asked Mark. It was the only thing she could think of. Either that or they were very highly strung.

"Maybe. They're sure not exercising discipline. Do you see the two against the west wall?"

West wall...Harper oriented herself in her head. The wide angle was at times hard to interpret. But yes, now she identified the two he was talking about. They were walking up and down the room aimlessly.

"They should be methodical. One pacing the perimeter, one with a weapon aimed at the hostages at all times. They're using up a lot of nervous energy. Give them three days and they'll be useless—exhausted and worked up, both. But we can't give them three days. Either they'll start shooting or the police will attempt a raid and the terrorists will be given advance notice. Either way, everyone will be dead at the end of it and probably the Louvre blown up. Including us."

She shivered and Mark put his arm around her shoulders. "That's not going to happen. And that's why we have to move tonight."

"At 3 a.m., when the body's defenses are weakest." She looked up at him.

Mark's eyes sharpened in the dim light. "That's right. How did you know that? Have you had counterterrorist training?"

"Not quite, but I do read a lot of thrillers. No, my grandfather passed away after a long battle with cancer at three in the morning. I was by his bedside. We were taking turns. I was holding his hand and something woke me up. I saw him take a deep breath and not breathe it out again. The doctor said that's when many sick and elderly people pass away. The body is at its lowest ebb."

He leaned over and kissed her hair. She felt it. Felt his big shoulder brush hers, felt his breath ruffle her hair, felt the light kiss, as if even her hair were attuned to him.

She closed her eyes and leaned into him for the kiss, drawing in a deep breath full of the scent of his skin. Her grandfather's last breath was still sharp in her memory as she'd watched life depart his ancient, desiccated body. She'd loved him, had tried to hold on to him, but he'd gone. She'd watched it, life leaving him.

Life hadn't left the body of the man beside her. Oh no. He was crackling with life, every inch of him.

And so was she.

In the midst of terrible danger, crazed lunatics parading with machine guns right outside this wall, hunkered down in a stone building that had been wired with explosives, she'd never felt so *alive*. Right down to her fingertips and toes. Every cell of her body hummed. Danger was so close, that thin veil that separates life from death almost visible, and yet she savored every single thing. Mark's closeness and strength like a bastion. The breath in her lungs, the shadows in the harsh light, the heat from Mark's body.

"So." Mark moved his head and spoke directly in her ear. She broke out in goose bumps. "When are you quitting your job and telling the boss from hell to go fu—jump in a lake. Next week, I hope."

She turned her head swiftly, meeting him nose to nose. "I'm so looking forward to telling him to fuck off."

Mark smiled, kissed her lightly on the lips. He tapped her chin. "Any woman who wants to leave relative safety to go out with me is not a woman who plays it safe. That's also not a woman who will put up with being mistreated. You're Wonder Woman."

Harper smiled. She liked the image of herself as Wonder Woman, marvelously brave. The fact was that she didn't want to be left alone in this dark, dusty space, waiting for Mark to come back. She'd rather face danger with him than tremble alone in the dark.

But she'd take his image of her—strong and unafraid. Felt good.

Mark nudged her with his shoulder. "So? What are your plans?"

"Are you sure you want to hear this?" Harper had some painful memories of talking about her work with dates. Not many men were interested in design.

His face sobered. He ran the back of his forefinger down her cheek. "Yes, absolutely. I want to hear what you do, what your plans are. I want to hear about people who care about beauty and art. I particularly want to hear this when there are terrorist thugs just feet away who have killed hundreds, maybe thousands of innocents and who want to blow up one of humanity's finest creations. I want to hear about people who can't even contemplate that kind of atrocity."

Even in the dim light, his eyes shone. They were locked on hers. All that formidable male energy was focused on her and it felt like being under a spotlight. He meant every word he said.

"Okay." Harper blew out a breath. Up till now she and her partners had treated their plans like nuclear secrets. Not even her parents knew everything. But that was in normal times. Normality had been blown out of the water and anyway, this was Mark. Either they were going to die tonight or if they lived, he was going to be part of her life.

Still, she hesitated, just a moment.

"Hard, huh?" Her head swiveled in surprise. He was smiling gently. "It's hard sometimes talking about the private stuff. I'm a vault," he added gently, lifting three fingers. "Scout's honor."

The man was scarily perceptive.

"Were you a Boy Scout?" Somehow, he didn't look like someone who'd been a scout. She imagined him as worldly as he was now, even as a boy. Like an old soul.

"No." The smile vanished. "But I know how to keep secrets."

He probably did. "Well, it's not a question of national security or anything. There are four of us—me, two young architects and a graphic artist. We're going to publish a large design magazine quarterly. The paper magazine will have high production values and we're hoping they will become collectors' items. We did a one-off test last year and it sold out in a week. Then the e-edition will have added content, podcasts, interviews, things like that. We've all sunk our life savings, such as they are, into the project and we're all going to resign from our day jobs next month."

"Good." Mark's mouth tightened. "Leave that jerk of a boss as soon as you can. I don't have many female employees, but when they travel, you can be sure there's a car and a driver waiting for them. No question."

He sounded so genuinely appalled that her boss begrudged her even taxi money. Harper remembered telling a date that she'd arrived in LA late at night in a torrential rainfall—what they called a river in the sky—and had to wait an hour for a bus, and he wasn't even listening. He'd responded by talking about an upcoming promotion. There hadn't been a second date.

"I think he'll be unhappy he chased me off."

"Losing you?" Mark picked up her hand, kissed the back of it. "Guy's gotta be insane."

"We've even got a company headquarters. My grandparents left me a big house on Chestnut Hill with a detached groundskeeper's house, which is perfect for us. The house is in disrepair and I don't have the money to fix it up, but the adjacent place is in decent shape. We're putting in a T3 line, turning one room into a cooled server room, redoing the electricity. It'll be perfect."

"It'll be a huge success." His voice sounded certain, the tone that of someone saying the sun will rise in the east tomorrow morning.

Harper smiled. "That's the idea. The first issue of the magazine will be devoted to the design of *Game of Thrones*. The costumes, the arms and armor, the sets. It'll be visually stunning."

Mark gave a little jolt and turned, eyes slightly widened. "*Game of Thrones*? Jesus, my favorite show. I'm obsessed with it. Save a copy of the first issue for me."

"Will do." Her heart warmed. She was a huge fan of *GoT* herself and the idea of dedicating the entire first issue to the design of the series had been hers. Now her partners were totally on board, wildly enthusiastic. "What's your favorite part?"

"Jaime's hand," he answered promptly.

"Jaime Lannister's *hand*?"

"Mmm. I had a teammate who lost a hand to an IED. That's an—"

"Improvised Explosive Device," she said quietly. She made a point of following the endless wars. Brave men and women were fighting for her, the least she could do was to understand their sacrifices.

"Yeah. Anyway, they gave him a miracle hand to replace it. An average man's grip is about 100 pounds but Greg's biomechanical hand's grip is over 300. Then he went and had a smith make a hand to fit over it that was just like Jaime Lannister's hand, and had it painted gold. Wears it when he goes to parties. His wife, well...she's a little bossy, and when he wears it he calls himself the Hand of the Queen." Mark's eyes gleamed.

Harper snickered. "I like him already."

"You'll meet him." Mark squeezed her hand. "When we get back home, we'll have dinner with him and his wife. You'll like her, too. Reya's very...lively. A lot of fun."

A hard hand gripped her heart and squeezed. Oh, how she hoped she could meet this Greg and his firecracker of a wife. Go out to dinner with them and have a good time. Go on dating the most fascinating man she'd ever met. See where this hot thing they had led.

They might never get that chance. Tonight could be their last night on this earth.

"Don't think like that," Mark said. He reached over and smoothed out the wrinkles between her eyebrows. "It doesn't go anywhere good. We're going to get out of this alive and we're going out to dinner with Greg and Reya sometime next week. Maybe the Barbary Coast. Would you like that?"

"Yeah." She barely got the word out through a tight throat. "Yes, I'd like that. I read the reviews. Sounds like a fabulous place."

"It is."

The Barbary Coast was a fairly new restaurant with Arabic décor and delicious Moroccan food. She'd been wanting to go for a while now but saving up for the project had been her priority.

And oh...to go with Mark and with his friends, who sounded like so much fun, people of substance, people of spirit. A man and a woman who hadn't let the loss of a hand get them down.

Oh God, she wanted that, so *much!* She wanted that light-hearted dinner at a great restaurant. She wanted a lot of evenings with Mark, getting to know him better, though she had a pretty good impression of what the core of him was like. The past twenty-four hours had been like being in a pressure cooker, but it had also shown her that he was good and brave. A real man.

And hot.

Because the sex they'd had was life itself and she wanted more of that, too.

She wanted to move forward *right now* with the magazine. Why wait? She'd waited way too long already. Her usual cautious approach to life...she had a good job, why give it up; the economic situation was uncertain; most start-ups failed in the first year...

What nonsense.

Life was meant to be lived to the fullest. You had to throw yourself forward, arms wide out. Life was so sweet, so rich, full of pleasures and, yes, pain. Pain meant you were alive.

Harper had so much and hadn't realized it. She loved her parents, she loved her friends, she loved design. She'd met a man she could love. Maybe...maybe already did love.

It could all be gone in an instant—tonight, in fact. Things could go wrong. The plan Mark had come up with, though a good one, could go crashing in a thousand ways. They could end up dead so easily, shot through the heart or the head by those monsters.

There was a thin veil between life and death and they were up against it.

Somehow Mark picked up on the thoughts racing through her head.

"It'll be okay," he said, arm tight around her shoulders. His strength and warmth seeped into her bones. "Let's set a date for the Barbary Coast. When are you flying back?"

She was startled. *When was she flying back?* What kind of a question was that? She might die tonight!

He smiled gently down at her and again, she had the feeling he was reading her mind.

"So?" He bent, kissed her forehead. "We're both busy people and we have to make plans. When's your flight back?"

"Tue-Tuesday," she stammered. "The tenth. And you? When are you flying back?"

"Tuesday," he said, matter of fact. "The tenth. Or whenever you fly back."

"What about your business?"

"I can take care of my business before Tuesday."

"And what is your business in Paris?"

Harper held her breath. She knew what Mark was definitely *not*. A plumbing supplies importer. But what *was* he—exactly? What was he in Paris for?

It was hard to tell in such faint light but that might actually be a slight smile she saw on Mark's face. "Not a hit, if that's what you were thinking."

Harper's breath whooshed out of her chest in relief and that definitely became a smile on his face.

"I'm a security expert, not a door-kicker or an assassin. I'm here to advise the director of Paribas Bank on their vault security."

Harper's eyes widened. Paribas was a big bank with vast resources. They could ask any consultant in the world for advice. If they'd chosen Mark—who was not French—then he must be one of the best in the world at what he did.

He hadn't given off that air at all, of being a world-renowned expert in his field. That was very clever of him, she realized. Keeping below the radar for the public at large.

"Can you still meet your commitments?" she asked, then realized that she'd bought into Mark's world view. They were going to get out of this mess alive, he was going to his meeting, they'd fly back to Boston together and have dinner next week at the Barbary Coast.

Felt good.

"Sure. Just like you're going to found your magazine. It's going to be a huge success, too."

"Thanks," she said softly. It was just what she needed—a morale boost.

"No, I don't want your thanks." Mark's face tightened, the harsh light deepening the grooves around his mouth, accentuating those high, hard cheekbones. A thousand years ago, he'd have been a chieftain rallying the troops before a battle and the light would have been a bonfire. "I want you to understand that we're getting out of this alive, that we're having dinner next week with Greg and his wife, and that you're leaving that crappy job as soon as you can."

And there it was again—that vision of the future. Of *a* future, bright with possibility, with him in it. Enticing and just there, not beyond her reach. All they had to do was survive the next 24 hours. That future felt bright and real and overcame the shadows of fear she had.

Mark settled, gently pushed her head on to his shoulder. "Rest. We've got hours of waiting ahead of us. Sleep a little, if you can."

Sleep? *Sleep?* With terrorists holding weapons on terrified hostages just a few yards away? With the Louvre wired to blow up and bury them in tons of stone?

Was he crazy?

"I know it sounds nuts," Mark said, keeping his hand on the side of her head, gently pressing, "but soldiers in the field sleep whenever possible. You don't know what's coming and you need to be as rested as you can."

Made sense, but Harper knew sleep would be impossible. "I'll try," she said, no conviction in her voice.

"Uh-huh." Mark turned his head to kiss her brow. "It would help if you closed your eyes."

"Not sleepy." She was so amped up. Not even a horse tranquilizer would put her to sleep.

"Close your eyes anyway."

Obediently, she shut her eyes, not that it would make any difference at all. She was way too wound up for sleep. No way.

In seconds, she plunged into a big, deep black hole of dreamless sleep.

Something jolted her awake and she opened her eyes suddenly, pulling in a deep breath. A large, hard hand covered her mouth and she struggled briefly, uselessly. Attempts to dislodge the hand were pointless.

She'd come out of sleep like a rocket shooting up into space, head spinning.

Where was she? Harper bolted up, a heavy weight dropping from her shoulders. It was dim, cramped, dusty. Where the hell...

Oh God. It all came crashing back. The Louvre, the attack.

Mark's satphone screen was blinking.

"You should get that," she whisper-croaked, throat raw.

Mark had been watching her keenly. But now that she was awake, he turned his attention to the satphone. He tapped his earbud. Listened for several minutes. "Roger," he whispered finally. He stood up in one fluid movement and held his hand out to her. It was amazing. He simply folded one leg under him and stood up. You needed amazing thigh muscles and abs to be able to do that.

She took his hand and creaked to her feet with a lot of help from Mark. Every muscle ached and her joints felt like someone had poured glue into them. How did he move so smoothly?

"Hi, Sleeping Beauty." He gave a crooked smile that made her heart thump hard.

"Hi." Harper frowned as some kind of schematic appeared on the satphone's screen, "What's that?"

"The mission, step one." He turned the screen so that she could see it. Harper took the satphone from him and studied it carefully. She didn't have a superb sense of direction and wasn't good at reading maps, but by turning it this way and that, she finally figured it out. A pulsing blue point helped. It was the endpoint.

"What's there?" Her finger covered the spot.

He pursed his lips. "What I asked for, I hope. Two canisters of carfentanyl, two gas masks, two sets of body armor, extra large and small, two noiseless pump mechanisms, a noiseless drill, an MP5 with six magazines, a Glock 19 with a holster and ammo, two Tasers and a can of knockout gas in case I have trouble on the way back, night-vision goggles. Dropped down a chimney."

Harper frowned as she traced a blue line from their current position to the blue point over and over. She cocked her head as she traced the line again.

He picked up on her mood. "Something wrong?"

Harper gave a sharp shake of her head. "I don't know. There's something...wait!" She pulled her cellphone out but it was dead. "Can you pull up my email address from your satphone? It's a Gmail address. h.kendall—"

"I know your email address," he said as he pulled up Gmail on the screen.

"How do you know my email address?"

"You gave me your card, remember? On the plane. That's how I knew your cellphone number."

Oh. Yes, she had. They'd exchanged cards and she'd completely forgotten that. She couldn't have recited his email address or cell number from memory if you'd put a gun to her head.

He pulled up Gmail and typed in her address.

"Password?" He handed it to her and looked away.

Harper typed in her password and pulled up her email feed. "Looking at what they sent you reminded me of something. It might be nothing, but if I remember correctly..."

She scrolled down, down, past hundreds of emails. Damn, she should purge more often... *there!* From didierrw@ya-hoo.fr. She scrolled down the long and gossipy message. "This was sent a week ago by Didier, a friend of mine who helped set up a temporary exhibit on the other side of the Louvre, the Richelieu Wing. But he had to coordinate with someone who works on this side and—here it is." She squinted to read the small print of the very long, highly detailed message recounting Didier's personal travails working with dunderheaded and unenlightened French bureaucrats. She translated for Mark's benefit. "So there I was, trying to overcome all this mad bureaucratic..." She stumbled.

"Shit," Mark offered. "Even I know that *merde* is shit."

"Right. Bureaucratic shit," she continued. "When in waltzes that moron Bertrand to say that the room will be closed for six months because a pipe broke."

"So that's that." Harper followed the line on the screen with her finger and tapped once on a spot before the line stopped at the pulsing blue dot. "There's the room they want you to go through but you can't because it's shut down and probably barricaded. Whoever gave you those schematics couldn't know about the closing of that room a week ago. You'd have to be an insider to know." She looked up at him. "You need me, Mark."

Mark shook his head, looked at the floor then back up at her. "Honey, we need to rethink this. You'd be better off staying here and waiting for me. I don't know how many terrorists are in the corridors and they're not tired enough to have lost focus." He cupped her face. "I couldn't live with myself if something happened to you. Please stay here."

A surge of panic rose, squeezing her heart.

"No!" She lowered her voice instantly. "No."

No, no, no.

No way was she staying here. The idea of cowering in the dark waiting for Mark to come back terrified her. A fear beyond words, beyond reason. Just the thought of it had her choking. With Mark, she felt safe. It was crazy, he wasn't Iron Man or Superman. He was an ordinary man, of flesh and blood. She'd seen his scars. He didn't have supernatural protection. He could be shot, wounded, killed.

But she'd rather be by his side in danger than alone. It was crazy, she knew that. But it was her deepest truth.

She was going with him.

Mark studied her face, watched her eyes. "You mean it," he said finally.

She nodded, throat too tight to talk. If he said no she'd have to steel herself not to grab the back of his jacket and simply hold on tight.

"It will be dangerous." He continued watching her.

She nodded. Yes, she knew that.

"Like I said before, you'd have to keep close to me at all times."

She nodded fervently. Of course.

"You do what I say, when I say it."

Her head just kept on bobbing.

"When I do this," he held up a tightly clenched fist, shoulder height, "you freeze."

"Colder than a popsicle." She nodded enthusiastically. God yes.

"You don't talk. Don't make a sound."

Instead of her head bobbing, she shook it violently side to side. No talking. Absolutely not. She crossed her fingers over her lips.

He continued looking at her, clearly weighing pros and cons. Whatever it was he decided didn't make any difference at all because she was coming with him, so she just waited.

"Okay," he finally said on a sigh. He wasn't enthusiastic and neither was she, but the alternative was staying in the darkness alone, terrified. Much better to be terrified, but with him.

Her breath whooshed out. She hadn't even realized she'd been holding it until her chest suddenly loosened with relief.

"One last thing." He blew out a breath. He clearly didn't want to say this but he had to. "I am almost certain that they wouldn't have left any living tourists out in the Gallery. Anyone left alive would just be a problem for them. They're already patrolling to deal with an attack by law enforcement."

Their eyes met, hers sad, his determined. He nodded sharply. "Still want to come with me?"

She nodded.

"Not happy about this," he warned her, jaw muscles clenching.

Okay. It didn't make any difference to Harper whether he was happy or not, just as long as she could go with him.

He hooked a big arm around her neck and pulled her toward him. She went into his arms naturally, chests meeting as if magnetized, as if she were made to be in his arms.

God yes. She snuggled there, completely safe as long as he was holding her. He held her long enough that the terrified trembling deep inside stilled, long enough for his body heat to warm her up a little.

They were going to do something very dangerous, but doing nothing was dangerous too. And they might just save a lot of lives.

Her lips curved. She rose on her toes, brought his head down so she could whisper into his ear.

"*Dracarys.*"

9

D*racarys.*
If Mark hadn't been so shit-scared of dragging Harper into battle, he'd have smiled. *Dracarys.* The warrior cry of Daenerys Targaryen atop her dragon. A golden-haired beauty riding straight into danger to destroy her enemies, shouting *"Dracarys!"*

Except of course, Daenerys had her dragons and Harper only had him. He'd protect her as fiercely as he knew how, but no one knew better than he did that shit happened. No matter how well prepared a soldier is, how much he trains, how well equipped, how well planned the attack, shit happens. He'd seen it with his own eyes. Stu Carrier blown up six hours before the helicopter that would take him back into the world was supposed to lift off. Sam Lawrence, agile as a mountain goat, putting a foot wrong, a cascade of rocks giving away his position and an enemy bullet finding his head. In the field, bad weather, bad juju, bad luck happened all the time.

And this wasn't a planned mission at all. He was operating solo, on the basis of a half-assed plan organized by a man he'd never met, and oh yeah, there was probably a mole operating in the ranks of the police.

Mark had no intel on how many terrorists were in the Gallery or posted throughout the wing. None. No one did. He was flying blind and oh shit, he was flying with Harper.

Taking her along went against every protective instinct he had. Though she was smart and agile and guaranteed to keep her cool, he didn't want her with him, he wanted her somewhere far away, safe and sound. A place where he could go to her when it was all over.

Yeah. If he could, he'd beam her straight to the Ritz where she could stay in his suite until he killed the bad guys and saved the hostages. If he could. And if he failed, well...everyone has to die sometime.

Except Harper. This was not her time to go. God, no.

But the thing was—she wasn't far away. She was here. And the choice was between being with him and facing danger or staying behind, but without him to protect her.

Crazy as it was, he'd rather she were by his side than alone. He'd tried to dissuade her but she felt just like he did.

He kissed her, sternly pushing away the thought that it might be the last time. No. No way. When this was over, they'd hole up in his suite, order food in, and stay in bed for three days. And he'd take care of his business, she'd do what she came to do, then they'd fly home together and they'd stay together.

They were going to have a lot of time. Forever, in fact.

But right now—*showtime.*

Mark reached down and slid out the slim ceramic knife from his boot seam. It wasn't a Ka-Bar, but it was razor sharp and easy to handle.

Harper froze, having forgotten that he'd told her he had a knife in his boot. Knowing it and seeing it were two different things. Would it freak her out? She looked at him narrow-eyed and gave a thumbs-up.

Fuck yeah. He liked that she was ferocious under that cool, classy exterior. She was going to need all the courage she could find, his *Khaleesi*. They were going blind into danger.

"Ready?" His voice the merest breath of sound.

"Ready," she said in a tone that couldn't be heard a foot away.

At least part of the way they could walk between the walls, out of sight. Mark tucked her behind him and started walking north. He knew she was staying behind him because he could feel the slight tug on the back of his jacket.

They headed out, following the light of the flashlight, walking between the walls around one room, two, three.

At the fourth room, Mark halted, held up his clenched fist. Harper immediately stopped behind him. They were at the beginning of the Gallery. The drop was across the intersection and down another corridor. They'd have to leave the protection of the walls, but first he had to see what was out there.

Mark dropped to one knee, pulling out his cellphone. Harper removed his backpack and took out the drill and cable connection. He nodded and applied the head of the drill to the wall.

It did its magic, except once the drill bit broke through, it was too dark to see much. But there was an app for that, and he thanked his lucky stars he'd hired his tech genius, Ralph. He tapped an icon on the screen and the view switched to night vision, a light, watery green.

Out in the wide corridor was a faint light. The terrorists had strung a few lights like Christmas lights operated by generators along the outside wall. It looked almost festive but it was anything but. Enough faint light penetrated the side rooms and augmented by night vision, it was enough to see by.

Harper's eyes widened and she held her thumb up again,

never taking her eyes from the screen. And she was the one who saw the patrolling terrorist. She tapped the screen, and at first he couldn't figure out what she wanted to say, but then saw the man dressed in black with an AK-47. His face was covered by a thick black beard that reached from just under his eyes to below his neck. He had small eyes and a jutting nose that had been broken at least once.

Beard or no beard, Mark wasn't going to forget that face.

They both watched the terrorist walk back and forth along the intersection. Mark counted paces, trying to figure out the fucker's guard rotation, when Harper tapped the back of his hand. She signaled moving the camera's view lower, to cover the floor. Mark rotated the camera and saw what she'd managed to see. Two huddled bodies on the floor in that boneless sprawl of death.

Bushy Beard was walking back from his patrol and kicked one of the bodies out of his way. The body lifted then flopped over. A young boy.

Mark stilled, white noise replacing strategic planning in his head. His muscles tensed and it felt like his skin would explode—

Harper clutched his arm and shook her head. *No.*

No, of course not. What was he thinking? Taking revenge for a boy who was already dead was crazy. Mark wasn't crazy.

But he looked carefully at Bushy Beard's face in the glowing green light that made the world look like it was underwater. Because that was a dead man walking.

Bushy Beard continued walking down the corridor toward the Gallery and disappeared from view. Mark timed it. Ten minutes went by before he walked back. A ten-minute patrol. Doable.

How many other guards were posted in this wing? Most of them would be in the *Mona Lisa* room, with the hostages. The rest were spread out through the building as insurance against a sudden storm of French SWAT. The bulk of them would be at the entrance.

The terrorists had hostages as deterrents, not to mention some of them would have remote detonators for the explosives, too. Though he doubted detonators had been handed to everyone. You don't give the power of massive destruction to foot soldiers. Mark had to operate on the assumption that the detonators would be held by the leader and maybe two or three others in the *Mona Lisa* room.

But there was no guarantee. They had to be really careful not to set off a massacre and destruction of one of humanity's greatest treasures.

No pressure.

Bushy Beard took off for another patrol, and Mark grabbed his satphone and drill and soundlessly opened the door. They slid out and he closed the door just as quietly. Bushy Beard didn't have night vision. They kept to the darkest shadows as they made their way down to the great intersection which was very dimly lit.

Thank God he'd asked for night-vision goggles with the other equipment. He'd be able to see better on the way back.

Mark had thought about asking for two sets of night-vision goggles, one for him and one for Harper. But what you saw in night vision was pale green and foreshortened. There was no depth perception, and it took time and training to move while wearing the goggles. He'd decided it was better for just him to have night vision and for Harper to stick close to him.

He observed the intersection for a moment, but no other patrolling terrorists came. The wing they'd invaded was a huge space and they had no reason to cover every square inch of it.

He looked back at Harper and pointed forward with his index finger. She nodded.

Good girl. Mark's chest swelled with pride. She looked frightened but determined, a good partner in every sense. As they moved forward in the shadows, they passed a room that had a barrier across the entrance and a huge painted canvas tarp attached to the perimeter of the entrance.

Breaking through would have cost time and could have attracted attention.

Harper tapped his shoulder, cocked a thumb at the barrier. The room they were supposed to go through. Mark nodded. They would head to the drop point through another room. But thanks to Harper's knowledge, they weren't going to waste time.

As they rounded another corner, there was a strong whiff of ammonia. Urine. He froze, pushed Harper back.

A terrorist had just finished pissing in a corner of one of the big rooms—a corner they'd all been using, considering the strong stench of urine—and was closing his pants. He and Harper were exposed. They couldn't get to any cover in the time it would take this guy to close his pants and look around. There was only one thing to do. The terrorist saw Mark rushing him, opened his mouth to shout, fumbling for the weapon hanging on a three-point sling around his neck.

But he didn't stand a chance. Not a fucking chance. He could have had a freaking nuclear weapon and it wouldn't have made any difference.

Mark closed the distance between them in less than a heartbeat, leading with the knife, punching it into the fucker's chest with one hand while holding his mouth shut with the other. He'd have gone for the throat—one fast, deep slice of the carotid artery—but they couldn't leave a blood trail.

Instead, he punched his knife right between the fourth and fifth rib and twisted, tearing the heart muscle. He moved his left hand to clasp the back of the terrorist's neck and pulled him close, so close he could hear the death rattle and see the light fade from the fucker's eyes.

The terrorist collapsed, held up only by Mark's hand around the back of his neck and his hold on the knife's haft.

Mark pulled the knife out and eased the dead man down. He couldn't see blood against the dark clothes but he could smell it.

"Pull my lock pick set out of my backpack," he said to Harper, and a second later it was in his hand. "Watch my back."

She turned and kept watch, head slowly swiveling back and forth. Mark opened the door into the wall, lifting the dead terrorist inside. He took a radio receiver from the terrorist's pants pockets and hefted the AK-47, stripping four magazines from waist pouches.

Man, it felt good to have firepower again.

He stepped out from the space between the walls and touched Harper's back. *I'm here.* She nodded without turning around. "No one has come by," she said, her voice so low it was almost soundless.

Good. Mark directed her to the entrance of the great room. They flattened their backs against the inside wall. Mark peeked around it into the corridor, not breathing, listening carefully.

All clear. They headed out carefully. His boots were designed specifically with soles that gripped but made no noise. Her shoes, too, were noiseless. She kept pace with him perfectly, step by step. *Good girl*, he thought again, wanting to kiss her.

No. *Fuck* no.

Very dangerous and very stupid to think of kissing a woman on a mission. Should never happen. But he'd never been emotionally involved on a mission before. Rightly so, because it was the pits.

It sucked. Rocks.

Half of him was terrified that something would happen to Harper. The other half was coolly determined to keep her safe. But the half that was terrified was dangerous. Not being sharp was the best way to get her hurt.

Never again. Never, *ever* again. If they got out of this alive, they'd go on vacation to Disneyworld and small, safe towns and never go anywhere dangerous. Though in this world, that was hard.

The big corridor was very dark, not having been strung with the Christmas lights of the Gallery. It was past midnight and through the big windows he could see the internal court-yard and the black hole where the Pyramid had once stood. Shards of glass gleamed in the moonlight, something of great beauty reduced to ruins.

Behind the black hole where the Pyramid had been was a seething mass of black bodies, police officers waiting for orders. In the distance, Mark could clearly see the light sources of cell-phone screens, far away from the jamming device.

They were massing, awaiting instructions. Knowing that a hostage situation could potentially last days.

And in their midst were traitors. A mole or moles ready to pass on information about countermeasures, maybe planning to get the terrorists away, certainly willing to kill the hostages and blow up the Louvre.

While the police were out there, awaiting orders, Robert's Special Forces men were climbing the steep rooftop to drop supplies. They would enter through a remote part of the museum and muster out of sight with suppressed weapons, waiting for the signal from Mark that the hostages and terror-ists were unconscious.

Then they could quietly eliminate the patrolling guards and make it to the hostages in the *Mona Lisa* room. Mark knew that though they'd have a lot of firepower and explosives, they would work hard to avoid damage to the Louvre and its works of art. They were French and the Louvre was sacred.

The mop-up of the patrol guards would have to be done quietly, one by one. No one knew who had the detonators, though Mark was certain that only the leader and two or three others had one.

That wasn't Mark's problem and it wasn't his mission. His mission was to put down the terrorists and hostages in the *Mona Lisa* room and to keep Harper safe.

They were at another intersection—a huge open space with no cover at all if a patrol came by. They'd be gunned down.

He lingered at the corner, indecisive. If it were just him, he'd make it across just as fast as he could and if he were discovered, he was now armed and he'd go down hard.

But he had Harper with him, who wasn't armed in any way and who would be caught in the crossfire. He looked as carefully as he could in each direction, knowing full well that the longer he waited, the greater the chance that a terrorist guard would come by on his rounds.

Goddamn. An image of a broken and bleeding Harper was keeping him frozen.

Shit!

He felt an urgent tap on his shoulder and turned half around to see an exasperated face and Harper rolling her index finger forward. That wasn't in the military manual of combat gestures but it was very clear.

Get going!

Stay with me, he mouthed and she nodded. One last long look in every direction and he took off. Harper followed right in his footsteps, completely silently, and they reached the other side of the intersection just as the sound of two pairs of boots came from the west corridor.

Two men, striding together in unison. Trained and alert. They marched as if on parade grounds. New recruits, true believers. Mark pulled Harper deeper into the shadows, retreating to the back of the nearest big room.

Mark hated doing it but he rushed them to the corner, where they stood with their backs against the wall. It was the darkest place in the dark room. Being backed into a corner was not good, physically or metaphorically, but there was no choice.

He could faintly discern the two terrorists standing at the opening ten feet apart, backs to the room, as still as statues.

God. Were their orders to stay there for the rest of the night? If that were so, Mark would have no choice but to rush them. He could take them down, no question, but he didn't know if he could do it completely silently. If they'd stuck together, he could have. But if they were going to stay apart, he was in trouble.

He could mow them down, but that would attract all the guards in the galleries and would be heard in the *Mona Lisa* room. The terrorists would start shooting and maybe press the detonator.

It was possible that they'd rigged the explosives in sections, able to blow up one part, leaving the room with the hostages intact, only even more difficult to reach.

Anything was possible.

Mark and Harper stood, breathing shallowly, backs against the wall, and waited. Mark glanced at his watch with the non-reflective surface once. He wouldn't do it again. Ten past midnight. He set off the stopwatch in his head and waited ten minutes, twenty.

The drop was going to be made at 1 a.m. He could even be late to it, but they'd expect some kind of signal that he'd picked up the load. Right now, he couldn't signal anyone or anything. If the two guards decided to spend the night there, they were fucked.

With the first morning light, he and Harper would be visible. Before that happened, he'd simply have to attack and kill them both, even if it brought the other guards running.

It would likely trigger a massacre of some of the hostages, lead the terrorists to blow up at least part of the Louvre.

This room had no internal walls, either. No hiding behind walls. No doors, nothing. Just a big empty space full of priceless paintings, with them in it.

Harper was completely still, her hand clenched on his left forearm. There was a loud squelch from a radio. She didn't jump but her hand tightened on his arm.

There was no reason for the terrorists to be quiet. The one on the right lifted his arm, presumably to press the 'talk' button on his chest rig.

"*Ma alkhata*?" he said, in Arabic. *What is it?*

This wasn't an encrypted comms set; the radio transmitted in the clear. *"Any news? Anything out of the ordinary?"*

"No. All clear."

Look behind you, buddy, Mark thought. *Not so clear after all.*

But neither of the men looked around.

Mark memorized the words, the intonation of the guard, certain that he could replicate it if he had to. He was a good mimic.

Harper's grip on his arm loosened.

So. Twenty minutes had gone by, meaning check-in by the terrorists patrolling the empty Louvre was not less than every twenty minutes. More likely, every half hour.

Mark stood absolutely still, but drops of sweat formed along his hairline, a drop trickling down his spine. He'd been a sniper and knew how to wait, but waiting here with Harper, knowing that if the guards turned around they couldn't outrun bullets, was the worst wait of his life. He could only imagine what she was going through, though she was utterly still by his side and didn't make a sound.

It felt like hours were going by.

Get out, he mentally commanded the guards. *Go patrol somewhere else.*

As if they'd heard him, they set off to the right.

He and Harper waited until the sounds of the guards' boots faded, and then quickly and quietly made their way to the entrance of the big room.

Though she made no sound, Mark felt Harper stiffen beside him. Her cheeks gleamed silver. Tears.

There were ten dead bodies in the corridor, each surrounded by a green lake of blood in his night vision. He'd seen them rushing in but she probably hadn't in the darkness. Three bodies were together, holding each other, a man, a woman and a child. And a man sprawled on top of a woman, trying to protect her even in his last moment of life. The rest had died alone, people who'd only wanted to see beautiful works of art, at the wrong time in the wrong place.

Mark had seen a lot of dead bodies in his life, and many civilian casualties, though there was something particularly affecting in these people, dead in a place that celebrated the best humanity had to offer, victims of the worst humanity had to offer.

The sight was probably devastating to Harper, so he was prepared to give her a second or two. But she surprised him by keeping pace without faltering once, though tears poured down her face.

Good girl, he thought for the millionth time. She was tougher than she looked.

They quietly made their way toward their goal. Robert's team would be making the drop and would have started staging for a counterattack, awaiting Mark's signal.

Finally, they made it to the huge room in the Richelieu Wing. On the west wall was an ornate fireplace with enormous wrought iron andirons. The room was a sort of a diorama of a 15th-century bedroom, with a surprisingly small canopied bed, a chest at the foot of the bed, and two tiny embroidered armchairs.

Mark went immediately to the empty fireplace. Robert's men knew the exact depth of the flue from the chimney pot and the length of rope was calibrated to stop right above the hearth. Nothing showed. No one would suspect that there was something there.

Moving fast, Mark pulled out his knife, reached up into the chimney and felt the big package. He yanked the rope and the package dropped a foot, allowing him to easily cut the rope. He caught the package and pulled it out. It smelled of rubber and soot.

There was no time to carefully unwrap. He slashed the dirty canvas packaging and pulled out the items they'd need, Harper by his side. He handed things to her, which she placed on the floor. First, two canisters that he handled very carefully. She picked up on what they were and handled them just as carefully as she placed them on the floor.

Their eyes met, hers full of determination. A close dose of what was in that canister would be instantly lethal, and she knew that, but she looked unafraid.

Jesus, what a woman. This was as far from her world as it was possible to get but she was proving to be as brave and resourceful as any of his teammates back in the day.

The pump that would soundlessly propel the knockout gas into the room. Weapon—ah. He slung the terrorist's AK-47 to his back and lovingly held the MP5 in his hands. Six magazines in the holders of a combat vest that would go over body armor. Plus, the Glock 19 with four magazines and a thigh holster. Both had fitted suppressors.

Two sets of gloves, just as he'd asked. One a pair of shooting gloves, and a pair of latex gloves for Harper.

Four flashbangs. They emitted overwhelming noise and light but did not explode. If this had been anywhere else, a couple of grenades would have been included. Robert hadn't even mentioned grenades.

Two gas masks. Mark checked them over very carefully. Any hole, even a pinprick, could prove fatal. But they looked brand new. He brought them both to his nose and they smelled new. If there was anything wrong with them and they died, Mark would come back to haunt Robert. Make his life miserable to the end of his days.

Body armor for Harper. That went on her immediately.

"Arms up," he whispered and her arms went up. He slid the two plates connected by shoulder straps over her head, then carefully tied the Velcro straps at the sides, making sure it covered her entire torso. It was big, so it did. It covered her from shoulders to below the pelvic area. She was protected from major injury.

Unless, of course, a shot caught her carotid or femoral arteries. Or both.

Or her head.

Fuck.

Mark bent and held her tightly, the body armor like a carapace around her heart. He was glad it was there but he couldn't feel *her*. Her warmth, her heartbeat. His head dropped to her shoulder.

She patted him on the back, as if to reassure him, calm him down.

Harper turned her head until her lips were right against his ear. "I'll be okay."

He nodded, hoping that was true.

"You'll make sure of it."

He nodded again, knowing *that* was true. By God, he'd do his best to keep her safe.

The satphone buzzed silently. He'd blacked out the screen. Robert, checking on him to see if he'd received the drop.

He had to let go of Harper, see to the next part of the mission.

His arms wouldn't obey him, he couldn't seem to let her go. Finally, it was Harper who stepped back. "Answer that," she whispered in his ear.

Yes. Mark wiped sweat from his brow and tapped the earbud.

"Did you receive the package?" Robert asked. Mark tapped his earbud twice.

"We're still staging, but we'll be ready by 3 a.m. Okay?"

He tapped twice.

"Good. *Bonne chance, mon ami.*"

Mark turned to find, to his surprise, Harper had picked up the rest of the equipment, wrapping it in the tarp he'd sliced open, carrying that over her shoulder.

He tried to take it from her but she shook her head and stepped back. "You have to keep your hands free," she whispered.

Mark's heart gave a sudden extra beat. He nodded and twirled his index finger.

Heading out.

10

The way back was as horrible as the way there, only harder. Harper was carrying all the equipment on her back, which made her feel unbalanced and awkward. Mark could have carried it laughing, together with her and probably a Volkswagen. But their one chance of survival if they were caught was Mark's ability with firearms and he needed his hands free for that. Luckily, he was now armed to the teeth with a submachine gun, another automatic weapon slung across his back which he'd taken from the dead terrorist, and some kind of pistol he wore on a holster. The weapons looked completely natural on him and he wore them as if they were invisible.

How could she have possibly mistaken this man for a boring businessman? Everything about him screamed *warrior*, unmistakably. The way he carried himself, ready for anything, the way he seemed to be aware of their surroundings at all times, his ability to plan a way to take down the terrorists without a massacre...wow.

He exuded power, it came off him in waves. Not political power or the power of money, which is what she was used to.

No, this man *was* power, in the old-fashioned sense of the term. An alpha male, in his prime, utterly dangerous.

Certainly, she was happier to be here in this impossibly dangerous situation with Mark Redmond, security expert, than she would be with Mark Redmond, plumbing supplies importer.

Harper followed Mark step by step, even when they had to go out into the great hall, full of bodies. It had sickened her when she'd first seen them, in that unmistakable sprawl of death. It still sickened her, the work of monsters.

But she couldn't react now, their job was to stop the terrorists from killing even more people.

She glanced at the bodies as they made their way quickly down the hall and sent up a silent prayer for their souls, gone too soon and gone too violently.

They reached the room where they'd taken refuge, the room the terrorists had used as a urinal. Mark glanced at his watch. It had a strange kind of dial that didn't reflect the light. Amazing. She'd never have thought of that. And yet a watch dial that gleamed was a dead giveaway.

They slid into the room, backs against the wall. That heavy bag of gear she was carrying slid silently to the ground.

She couldn't see them, but she knew that the room was filled with masterpieces. Works of art that had inspired millions but that could be destroyed at any minute. One monster pressing a detonator and they would be lost forever, together with the lives of the hostages, and their own lives. She had no idea how a human being could do that but she also had no idea how they could have shot those innocent tourists.

This wasn't humanity as she knew it. These were beasts, monsters.

This was what Mark did. Fight monsters.

As if he knew she was thinking about him, he turned his head with those weird goggles that made him look like an alien insect. It was too dark to see his expression but he held up his thumb.

Everything okay?

You didn't need to be a soldier to understand it. She lifted her own thumb.

Everything's peachy.

Her back and knees hurt from carrying all that weight. She was exhausted and filthy and terrified, but damned if she'd show him that. He was brave, so by God, she was going to be brave too. Or at least pretend to be.

He nodded, and she could see that he'd dismissed her from his mind. Damn right. She didn't want to be a distraction or burden in any way. If they were going to get out of this alive, if they had any hope of saving those hostages and saving the Louvre, it was all on Mark. On his combat skills, intelligence, instincts, focus. His bravery.

He was studying his watch and swiveled his head toward her. What was he trying to communicate…?

Oh. The two guards were coming back, boot heels clicking loudly on the parquet flooring. They didn't have to be silent. They thought they'd already won.

Think again, you sons of bitches.

She surprised herself with the red, raw rush of hatred that rose up and clouded her mind for a moment. She'd have strangled them with her bare hands at that moment if she could.

But she couldn't. She could only be as silent as possible and wait for them to go away, back on patrol.

If she understood correctly, an army of commandos was gathering, ready to take the terrorists down as soon as she and Mark released the gas in the *Mona Lisa* Room. They were going to have to be fast and brutal, so no one had a chance to set off the explosives.

But the first line of defense here, the one indispensable

person, was Mark. He was the one who was going to make that rush possible.

She reached out unconsciously to touch his arm, reassure herself. He was so silent she could only know he was there in the darkness by his body heat, by the denser darkness that was Mark.

He picked up her gloved hand, brought it to his mouth and kissed it without looking at her.

It was like an infusion of power, a sudden rush of it. Power and heat racing through her body, light in darkness.

They waited for what felt like forever but was probably only ten minutes. The concept of time was gone. There was no light to see her watch. The feeble light in the corridor barely penetrated the opening of the room.

Her heartbeat was no longer a timekeeper. Hers was racing, irregular and fast. All she knew was that it felt like she was suffocating in the timeless darkness as they stood frozen. Mark didn't move a muscle, so neither did she. The two terrorists would have had to move into the room and pace the perimeter to find them.

They didn't do that. They stood at the entrance, backs to the room, and exchanged quiet words.

Suddenly there was a loud squawking sound that made her jump a little. Mark touched her arm reassuringly and she was ashamed of herself. It was only their radio or walkie-talkie. One of the terrorists moved his arm and spoke quietly into the receiver. A minute later, they walked back out into the corridor, back on their rounds.

She let out her breath in a silent whoosh, unaware that she'd been barely breathing. Mark held up a hand, listening hard. When they couldn't hear the boot steps, they moved quietly to the entrance and out into the big corridor, across the intersection, into the Gallery.

One big room, two, three. Finally, they reached the room

where they could enter the walls and continue to the *Mona Lisa* room undetected. Mark moved right to the side wall and took out his lock-pick set.

He was working fast, unable to completely muffle the small metallic sounds of the lock pick working its magic.

Two men's voices sounded out in the Gallery and Harper tapped frantically at his shoulder. Mark nodded but otherwise gave no sign of urgency, merely continued working at the lock.

The voices were becoming louder.

They were shielded by the darkness but not completely hidden. If one or both of the patrolling terrorists had very keen hearing and decided to look in, they'd see two shadows darker than the night.

Mark couldn't keep watch, all his attention was taken up with the lock, so it was up to her to be his lookout. She turned her back to the wall and stared with every ounce of attention at the entrance, a slightly lighter shade of dark.

The voices grew even louder. They weren't speaking loudly, she knew that. It just felt loud, the voices seemingly impinging on her skin. If they were discovered, they wouldn't be the only ones to die. It might actually trigger the massacre of the hostages, the detonation of the explosives.

God, no.

She wanted to whisper *hurry!* to Mark but that would be useless and distracting. Mark was working as fast as anyone could. He knew the dangers and the risks. His hands were steady from what she could hear in the gloom.

A last light click of the lock and the door swung open—just as the two terrorists made it to the entrance of the room. She could tell because of the echoing sound their voices made. They were exactly opposite them, in full view if there was light. She hunched her shoulders and tensed her muscles, which would be amazingly useful against machine-gun fire.

The sound of the terrorists' boots came loud and clear and

Mark ushered her in with a strong hand on her shoulder. He followed her immediately and shut the door soundlessly with not a second to spare.

Harper thought her heart would hammer its way out of her chest. It was completely lightless inside the wall but she dropped the bag stepped into his arms without hesitation as if they were in broad daylight. Once again magnetic, their two bodies coming together unerringly with an audible click, the two sets of body armor meeting.

Harper burrowed, holding Mark tightly, wondering if he could hear her hammering heart shaking against the armor. She trembled and he held her more tightly, as if he could absorb her shock and sorrow and, yes, terror.

It worked. Embracing the heat and strength of his strong, hard body somehow transmitted something—courage? hope? —to her, and the trembling died down. She could draw in a breath that wasn't painful. Her jaws unclenched. Her heart stopped trip-hammering and began beating steadily.

Her arms relaxed. She held him instead of clutching him.

Mark's head bent down to her. The scruff of beard he'd developed itched against her cheek and she welcomed the small bite of it. It grounded her.

"Okay?" he whispered in her ear and she nodded, stepping back. A little ashamed, but not too much. He'd just lent her a little bit of his bravery.

Mark led them both farther down the corridor between the walls, far from the door he'd opened, and he pulled out the flashlight. His arm rose up and she felt more than saw him remove the goggles and then switch on the light.

The narrow beam was bright after the darkness and she blinked.

"Give yourself a minute and let your eyes adjust to the light," he said, voice low. She nodded, watching him as he slowly came into focus, seeing his face again clearly after the hour of semi-darkness.

Strong cheekbones, clean features, slight beard.

In the past hour, he'd killed a man and saved her life, safely brought them to the drop-off point and back, and was now going to save the lives of the hostages.

"What?" he asked, dark eyebrows drawing together in a frown.

"You're magnificent," she whispered, and rose up on her toes to kiss his cheek.

"Nice to know," he whispered back. "Say that to me again when it's over."

There was nothing to smile at. They were in deadly danger. Murdered men and women were outside in the Gallery terrorists were holding over a hundred hostages at gunpoint. But she smiled anyway.

"You betcha."

11

Here is where it got tricky.

Now that they were inside the walls, Mark put the Glock in his holster and picked up the improvised sack of combat goodies from the floor. It wasn't heavy for him but it must have been staggeringly heavy for her, not that she'd complained.

Not for one second.

He remembered Evers on patrol. Evers hated carrying things. He'd have bitched endlessly about hauling around a big bulky bag over his shoulder while avoiding armed guards.

Not Harper. She was the real deal.

She didn't complain that he'd taken the weight now, though.

Now they had three big rooms to get across between the walls and they had to do it quietly. It was early morning. Any guards who were awake would be hypersensitive to noise in the quiet of the deepest part of the night.

Mark held a finger up to his lips and she nodded. Not that she'd made any noise up until now, but still. Now it was doubly important that no one discover their existence. Hundreds of lives and maybe the very existence of the Louvre itself depended on it. Not to mention their own lives.

They were going to make their way slowly and carefully.

Mark set off, his flashlight reduced to a small point, just enough to show where the walls were and the floor in front of them. Just enough light to ensure that they didn't trip.

Again, she held on to him. Finger curled into one of the empty pouches of his combat vest. She stepped so lightly in his wake that he could barely feel her, but felt reassured that she was there, following him step by step.

They made their way slowly around the big rooms, between the walls, until they reached the *Mona Lisa* room.

Mark knelt and fixed his smart phone to the USB end of the cable he'd left in place and tapped the screen. The tiny camera had night vision and infrared, which he didn't need at the moment. The night vision gave a clear picture though the light in the room was dim. The hostages were massed in the middle of the room. Most of them were slumped in sleep, the kids in their mothers' or fathers' arms, a few sprawled on the floor. Several of the male hostages were upright and awake, but there was no chance of rushing the terrorists ringing the room. Some of the hostages might be waiting for an opportunity to present itself but it would never come. Even if, by some miracle, they managed to overcome the guards in the room, the patrols would come rushing in, shooting.

Sorry guys, Mark wished he could say. *I know you want to kill these fuckers but you can't. Let me take care of it.*

The guards here were alert, rifles in their hands, pointed at the floor. But it would take only one second for those rifles to be shouldered. And for that matter, they could shoot from the hip. The center of the room was a target-rich area if ever there was one. Even shooting from the hip, they couldn't miss with automatic weapons.

A baby suddenly started crying and he could hear the

mother desperately trying to stifle the cries. The nearest guard raised his rifle threateningly. It was not so dark that the hostages couldn't see the guard shouldering his rifle.

The mother was panting and moaning in terror. A man—presumably the father—scrambled inside a backpack and came out with a baby bottle, which he put in the baby's mouth. The crying stopped instantly and after a moment, the guard let his rifle drop and stepped back.

There was an audible whoosh of relief from the hostages.

Damn! That little drama was going to make the terrorists more aware, even more alert. If Mark could, he'd wait another hour to make sure that boredom could descend on them once again, but he didn't have an hour.

The police were massed outside on the great concourse, probably spilling out onto the avenue along the Seine. With a mole who was reporting to the terrorists. Their leader would know that no action was being taken for the moment.

Wrong.

Because Robert's commandos were preparing to infiltrate, half through the roof and half through the bombed entrance via an underground tunnel, and they were waiting for Mark's command. Once Mark reported that the men holding guns on the hostages were unconscious, the commandos would come rushing in with suppressed weapons, shooting their way to the *Mona Lisa* room. It would be up to Mark to take care of any guards who came rushing toward the hostages.

It was going to be tricky and hard keeping everyone safe. And Mark had an overriding concern—keeping Harper safe. Because he wanted to survive this mission and he wanted Harper in his life. He wanted that badly.

He lifted his gaze from the screen and looked at her. She was standing quietly, carefully watching him. Looking to him for clues as to what to do. This wasn't her world, but she knew it was his and was willing to follow his lead.

An amazing woman.

He'd given her the flashlight to hold, the light facing up. It created a dim, suffused light reflected off the ceiling.

He bent his head, speaking directly in her ear. "I'm going to put the gas mask on you. Do you suffer from claustrophobia?"

She shook her head, then nodded. "Only in crowds."

"Good. It'll be really uncomfortable. Very hot. Hard to breathe, hard to see. You'll be tempted to shift it around to make it more comfortable, but don't touch it. There's no peripheral vision, you'll have to turn your head to see things to the side. It's very isolating and it will muffle your hearing. Are we clear on that?" Some soldiers suffered from mask phobia and tore their masks off in the stress of battle.

She nodded, eyes huge in her face.

"You'll hear your own breathing and it will sound weird. Like Darth Vader. So. This is what will happen. I'm going to gas the room, both sides. I really don't know how long it will take to make everyone unconscious, and Robert didn't know either. So we'll wait. I'm going to crack open the door, this one that opens directly into the *Mona Lisa* room, and be ready. When I give the signal, the French Special Forces guys are going to be rushing into the building, up the grand staircase and down toward the Gallery. Some will drop down through that chimney. They're all going to be moving as fast and as silently as possible. If things go well, they'll be here in a few minutes. You'll stay inside the wall."

"Okay." She nodded again.

"But—sometimes shit happens." He had to prepare her for that, too. Actually, shit happened more often than not. "If the SF guys don't get here in time, or the guards are conscious enough to start shooting, I'll have to intervene. If that happens, I want you to *stay inside*. Close this door quietly and run to the next room through the walls. Run away from this room and then lie down on the floor, as flat as you can. Is that clear?"

God, if it turned into a live-fire situation, he didn't know if these walls would provide sufficient cover. The thought of a bullet hitting her—he couldn't go there.

"Yes."

"Repeat what I said."

A tenet of soldiering. In the heat of battle, sometimes people froze. They developed tunnel vision and couldn't think straight. That's why soldiers repeated orders twice. Pilots, too.

"After you pump gas in the room, we wait. If a situation arises where you have to go out, I run to the next room and lie flat on the floor."

"Excellent." He kissed her cheek. His brave soldier.

Suddenly, Harper grasped his body armor at the top and yanked hard until they were nose to nose. "Don't go into that room unless you absolutely have to. Don't be a hero and get yourself shot."

She was fierce, eyes a blazing gray that shot rays of power. Her nostrils flared and there were white lines around her mouth. Power crackled from her. She was magnificent, this classy woman who cared deeply about design.

"Yes, ma'am," he said, and kissed her.

She threw her arms around his neck and kissed him back, hard. Holding him as tightly as she could, mouth open, devouring him. And he was devouring her, the kiss rough and desperate. It wasn't about sex, it was about connection, bonding, saying all those things that couldn't be said in words.

Don't get yourself killed.

I won't.

I think I love you.

I think I love you too.

He tasted her desperation, her fear, her courage. No tears, just a tight hold on him because they both knew it might be their last kiss. It might be a kiss that had to last a lifetime.

Harper clutched at his neck, wanting to get closer, but they both had body armor on so they were touching each other where they could reach skin. He had his hands clasped around her head, soft hair falling over his wrists, soft mouth crushed under his.

He was hard as a rock, mostly desire to possess this woman once more because it might be the last time, but a small part of it was combat adrenaline, the male body wanting to celebrate life right in the moment in which life might depart the body. And maybe some thousand-year-old instinct to impregnate before death—throwing yourself into the next generation even if you wouldn't be there yourself.

Who knew?

All he knew was that he'd give a limb for the chance to have sex with her again, right now.

But he couldn't, and the part of his brain that was a modern warrior overcame the bigger part of his brain that was a primitive warrior. He pulled away from her mouth with a devastating feeling of loss.

Their foreheads met. Looking down, Mark could see her impossibly thick lashes concealing her eyes, a silvery track left by a tear that was no longer visible. Harper's breath came fast and sharp, as if she'd been running.

"Gotta do it now, honey." He kept his voice cool and even.

She swallowed, nodded.

"But first I have to fit the gas mask on you."

"Okay."

"You won't like it," he warned.

"There's a lot of things I don't like," she said, lips curved slightly in a smile as she met his eyes. "But I do them anyway."

Yeah. He was the same way.

Mark reached down for a mask and held it up so she could see it. If she freaked, he didn't know what he'd do, because she was going to wear it, no matter what.

She was going to stay within these walls, but Mark had no

idea if the gas would seep through. Had no idea of the dosage, if someone who knew what they were doing had calculated strength according to the volume of air in the room. Maybe not. The Louvre authorities would know exactly how big this room was, how big the entrance to the Gallery was, but those people wouldn't be the people who'd put together the canisters.

This was a top-secret mission, no one on Robert's team would have called up a Louvre administrator to query the exact measurements. Knowledge of the strength of the gas would have had to be inside the wheelhouse of Robert's team. This entire rescue had been organized in a couple of hours by people who were experts on violence but not biochemistry.

He hated to admit it, but the carfentanyl had a strength that could kill. Carfentanyl was 10,000 times more potent than morphine. He was absolutely certain that the French Special Forces would have done their best, but...shit happens.

A big dose of carfentanyl could stop a charging rhino in its tracks.

So, Harper's life was in the hands of people he didn't know and couldn't vouch for, except in the vaguest of terms.

She'd be wearing the mask and she'd keep it on until they were safe and sound.

Mark carefully fit Harper's mask. It wasn't sized for a woman. They'd simply thrown in two masks from military stock. It was too large for her small face and he had to tighten the straps at the back of the head in a way he knew would be uncomfortable for her, and hope to God nothing penetrated.

Once it was tightly fitted, he stepped back. Like everyone wearing a gas mask, she looked like an alien. "How is it?" he asked.

She held up her thumb.

Yeah, right.

But she wasn't fighting it, wasn't touching it.

Okay, now for his own. He put on the mask, making sure

the rubber seal was intact. He hoped to God that France didn't have a system where government bureaucrats awarded contracts to the lowest bidder.

The masks didn't have night-vision capability so he had to keep the light on, but low. Harper held the flashlight, on its lowest setting and pointed to the ceiling.

She held the light steady. He pointed at the baseboard and she obediently held it there, rock steady. The area he was going to work in was lit by a dull light, barely enough to see what he was doing.

Mark walked a meter down and pulled out a silent high-speed drill, calibrated to drill a hole the size of the gas tube. The drill head was pushed against the wall and he switched it on, wincing. But Robert had come through. It was silent.

Inside a minute, he was through. The drill head was a matte black. In the darkness of the room, it wouldn't be seen.

He pulled his cell toward him, studying the screen for several minutes. Nothing changed, no one sounded the alarm. He looked up at Harper and she nodded agreement.

So far so good.

They walked through the walls to the other side of the *Mona Lisa* room where he repeated the drilling sequence and fit the canister tube in. The canisters had a timer and he set the timer for three minutes and rushed Harper back to their original position.

He checked his watch for the countdown and at three minutes minus ten seconds, signaled to Harper to turn the flashlight off, then fitted the canister pipe to the hole in the wall by touch. It slid in perfectly, with no clearance around it.

"On," he whispered through the gas mask, and she switched the light back on, barely illuminating the area.

He looked up at her, hand on the gas canister switch, hoping to God they'd given him a silent pump. If it gave off the sound of compressed air and the terrorists heard it before succumbing, he and Harper were already dead.

Now.

He turned the lever and it was silent. He breathed out, switching his attention between the screen showing the room and the gas level indicator.

When the level indicator reached one quarter, Mark tapped his ear twice and heard a muffled *"Allez!"* through the earbud. Robert had given the go command.

The Louvre was now under counterattack.

Ambulances had been waiting along the Seine and could now rush to the staging area. Mark could hear sirens faintly, becoming louder as they came closer. The medical personnel would have preloaded syringes full of an antidote to the carfentanyl, to be administered to kids and thin adults first. Hospitals had been told to expect incoming patients.

And right now, maybe a hundred Special Forces commandos were dropping from the roof and rushing the entrance of the Louvre with silenced weapons.

So much activity, yet here in the room itself, silence reigned.

And there—the first terrorist to fall. The terrorists ringing the walls were the closest to the gas. One of the guards rocked on his boot heels then collapsed. And another.

A very thin woman who'd been sitting cross-legged on the outer edge of the group just keeled over. Then two men facing each other toppled forward, torsos touching each other, upright but unconscious. Then a couple just sprawled to the floor as if falling asleep really fast. It was hard to tell with the kids, because most of them had been asleep on an adult's lap. But the adults, they were succumbing.

Two more guards fell suddenly, as if they were puppets on a string and their strings had been cut.

One guard looked alarmed, bringing up his weapon, mouth

open for a shout. Mark tensed, then the guard fell. He was heavy-set, the gas taking longer to put him down.

After a minute, two, everyone in the room was down. Two of the guards had fallen noisily, their guns clattering. The rest slumped to the ground.

Excellent. The whole thing had been almost soundless, except for the squawk from their internal comms units. Faint noise was coming from the corridor, the commandos doing their best to be noiseless, but battle was noise and confusion. Always had been, always would be, until battle became a battle between computers.

For now, battle was human and there was some noise.

Fuck! Two guards from the corridor were checking in. They ran, their boot heels loud in the corridor, sliding to a stop at the entrance to the *Mona Lisa* room.

They were quick. Both took in the situation, took in their men down, knowing this was an emergency, knowing that this was their last chance to effect a massacre.

Mark knew enough of the mindset of men like this to know that, to them, an end to the situation without more dead was a loss. He shouldered his weapon, pushing down the lever to open the door into the *Mona Lisa* room to go fight the next battle in the endless war of monsters vs. humans.

He was checked by a tug on his jacket.

"You're going out there?" Harper whispered, eyes wide. Her voice had the metallic tone of a mechanical voice.

Hurry. That was a drumbeat in his head.

"Yeah," he whispered back. "Have to, honey."

"Dracarys," she whispered. "Kill them all."

"Dracarys."

And he slipped out the door.

12

One minute, Mark was there, the next he was gone, swallowed up in the dim light.

Harper held his cellphone, watching the screen as if her life depended on it. And in a way, it did.

Everybody had slumped within a minute or two of the gas being pumped into the room. She understood very well that it was powerful, even dangerous, and was grateful for the mask, though it was fiercely uncomfortable.

A small price to pay for remaining conscious. Except she had to watch Mark go into war, which was hard. The instant he saw the two terrorists appear at the entrance to the big room, he moved to enter it. She had a side view of him, halfway across the room, big body in a crouch, gun with a silencer—what he'd called a suppressor—held in front of him in a two-handed grip.

The two terrorists were far apart, which she instinctively knew was bad news. He'd have to shoot fast and true.

She heard a coughing sound and the terrorist on the right flew backwards, holding his shoulder, then another coughing sound and the terrorist on the left simply crumpled, shot at the hip.

She couldn't hear anyone else in the corridor running, so maybe...

Something...something was moving. At the opposite end of the room, under the *Mona Lisa*. Mark was now at the entrance, peering both ways, seeing if other terrorists were coming, but behind him was movement.

The lead terrorist, who had a black scarf covering his nose and mouth, was stirring. He moved slowly, as if in pain, eyes half closed. But then with a huge effort, he raised his submachine gun...

He was going to shoot Mark!

She'd read somewhere that pulling a trigger took as much effort as popping the ring on a can of beer. Almost nothing. The man was moving very slowly, not quite out cold, but if his finger was on the trigger, he could strafe the room and hit Mark. The terrorist wouldn't care at all if his bullets also hit some of the hostages.

She wore the latex gloves, which were too big and had ripped where they caught on the equipment she'd handled. They were in her way, and she tore them off and opened the door.

There was no time to yell to Mark, there was no time to do anything but rush out of the room. She was only steps away from the terrorist. She stooped to snatch the weapon of one of the guards on the floor. The machine gun had flown from his hands and was lying on the hardwood floor. She scooped it up, feet flying.

For a second, she thought of using it as a gun, but she didn't know anything about guns. In the movies, you had to cock a gun, or slide something forward or backward, or do something...there was no time to study the mechanism for firing and she wasn't sure she wouldn't knock herself on her backside if she did.

So firing was out. But the butt was solid metal and would make a fine weapon.

These thoughts ran through her head so slowly while her body moved as fast as it possibly could.

Out the door, snatching the gun from the floor, running on silent feet to the head terrorist, holding the gun by the barrel, watching him slowly turn his head, the whites of his eyes visible in the dark room, his clumsy struggle to change the direction of his gun barrel...

But it was too late because with one last push of her foot, she was there, right above him, filled with rage and a ferocious protectiveness—*he was not going to kill Mark!*

And she pulled her arms back and swung the butt of the rifle against his head—and rejoiced when she heard a distinct *crack!*

One crack, then two as his head bounced on the floor.

She didn't know whether he was alive or dead, and she didn't care. The important thing was that Mark was safe. She checked the entrance to make sure he was okay—but he wasn't there.

Where...

God, had that asshole terrorist got off a shot anyway? How could that be? She hadn't heard anything!

Was Mark right now lying in a puddle of his own blood?

Harper started toward the entrance—but something held her back.

She struggled mightily, trying to turn the gun around to shoot whoever was stopping her from making it to Mark, when she heard a metallic but familiar voice.

"That's enough, superwoman." A big hand appeared in the narrow field of vision the gas mask afforded and lifted the weapon from her lifeless fingers.

Everything came crashing down. She stopped moving, but it felt like her insides were still traveling at a million miles an hour. Every cell in her body tingled and felt numb at the same time. Her legs wobbled. She looked around for something to sit on but there was nothing. Maybe she could just collapse to the floor...

A strong arm went around her waist and she leaned into him, trying to breathe him in even though the only thing she could smell was the rubber of the gas mask. She fumbled at the straps and he blocked her hands.

"Not so fast, Daenerys. The gas is still potent and it'll knock you out." He pulled her into his arms, held her tight. He bent his head and their masks knocked together. "I lost about ten years off my life when I saw you head out the door and make for that fucker. That *armed* fucker. What on earth possessed you? What were you thinking?"

She had no idea what she'd been thinking. The truth was, she hadn't been thinking at all, just feeling. Rage and terror at the thought that the head terrorist would fell Mark.

She pushed against him feebly, trying to put outrage into her voice, which came out muffled and metallic. "I just saved your life! A little gratitude here."

He sighed, the sound coming out as if from the bottom of a well. "You did save my life, but then I nearly died of a heart attack when I saw you running toward him, so it's a wash."

"It is *not* a wash!" She pushed against him again, but it was pointless. He was holding her tightly and his grip was strong. "I'll have you know—"

She stopped. Even through the mask, there was the sound of a few shots and running feet. Mark immediately let her go, took her arm and ushered her back into the wall, closing the door behind them just as a number of men rushed into the room.

They both hunched over the cellphone screen. At least twenty soldiers rushed into the room, heavily armed, dressed in black combat gear and with gas masks. They all had combat rifles tightly fitted to their shoulders. One of the soldiers set up a big halogen lamp and the room was suddenly illuminated bright as day.

It was an apocalyptic scene—the hundred or so hostages unconscious, in a heap in the middle of the room, the fallen terrorists around the perimeter.

Four soldiers were deployed as guards along the walls and at the entrance and they kept their rifles at their shoulders, body language showing they were ready for anything. The other soldiers let their weapons drop and started putting flex cuffs on the terrorists' wrists and ankles. Inside of a minute or two, they were all immobilized.

One of the soldiers tapped his shoulder and spoke into a built-in microphone.

Before Mark could ask her to interpret, Harper murmured, "He's reporting that the terrorists are under control, that they have cleared the Grand Gallery, and to send in medical personnel." She looked up. "Do they know we're here?"

"They know someone was here. Robert knows we're here, we'll be evacuated shortly."

Okay. Harper trusted Mark's judgment.

They waited quietly, watching the screen. The French Special Forces soldiers were efficient. They must have taken care of all the terrorists one way or another because no one even attempted an attack. They dragged the terrorists out into the Grand Gallery and arranged them like logs, then started evacuating the hostages, starting with the children.

"The quicker they can get the hostages away from the gas, the quicker they will recover," Mark said, and she nodded.

Masked medical personnel came running and piled the hostages onto gurneys, sometimes two or three at a time. The children, in particular, were loaded onto the gurneys with their mothers. There were a lot of hostages but they'd come prepared and worked fast. In less than a quarter of an hour, all the hostages were gone as were the terrorists outside in the Gallery.

Soldiers were still milling around, gathering evidence, pulling bullets out of the walls. The room with the *Mona Lisa* was now a crime scene.

A broad-shouldered man dressed in a suit and overcoat instead of combat gear, but wearing a gas mask, broke away from talking with the French commandos and walked directly to their door. The way the camera was set up, he loomed like a big-headed monster by the time they heard two sharp raps.

Mark opened the door a crack and the big man slipped through. He wasn't as tall as Mark but was broad-chested and held himself like Mark. Like a soldier.

"Robert?" Mark held out his gloved hand.

It was caught in the other man's gloved hand. "Redmond, I assume."

Mark nodded and watched as the man brought out a small wand made of steel and plastic. It had a small indicator inset in the steel. He nodded and peeled off his mask, revealing a tough, almost brutal face.

"There is a negligible amount of gas in here," he said. "We can remove our masks."

Mark took his mask off—then stood astounded as Robert gave him a huge hug and kissed him on both cheeks. *"Mon ami!"* he cried. *"Vous nous avez sauvés!"*

"You've saved us," Harper translated helpfully, amused as hell at the expression on Mark's face. It was hard to look both astounded and embarrassed, but he managed it. She took off her own mask and breathed in deeply. God, it was good to smell air, even dusty and dirty, as opposed to rubber. The mask had made her feel as if she were choking instead of breathing.

However, it had also kept her from being gassed. There was that.

Robert was holding Mark's shoulders tightly, beaming a smile up at him. Clearly, Mark was afraid he'd kiss him again.

Harper came to the rescue. She touched Robert's arm and said in French, "*Monsieur*, can we get away from here? I-I'm feeling faint." To add to the lie, she closed her eyes and slumped a little.

Wrong. She felt fine. She felt more than fine. They'd done the impossible and saved over a hundred lives. They'd saved the *Louvre*. She was tired but she was also revved. She wanted to sleep for a hundred years and she wanted to eat cake and drink champagne.

Both. Right now.

"*Mais oui, mademoiselle!*" Robert exclaimed. "*Avec plaisir.*" He offered his arm and she took it with a secretive wink at Mark.

Robert took out two ski masks, handing one out to Harper and one to Mark. She looked questioningly at the black wool mask in her hand.

Mark took it from her and slipped it over her head, tucking in her hair. It was scratchy and, frankly, a little smelly. Better than the gas mask but not by much.

He took her shoulders again. "Honey," he said, his voice low and serious. "We're going to make our way out through a side entrance, but make no mistake, the building is surrounded by every journalist in Paris, plus a billion people with cellphones. It's going to be a media circus. We're going to try to avoid as many people as possible, but you never know. So keep that thing on, are we clear?"

Absolutely. She nodded. Mark raised his eyes to Robert and circled his index finger, apparently a universally understood gesture among soldiers.

They made their way quietly inside the walls in a little convoy, Harper sandwiched between the two large men, following their lead. Not too fast and not too slow, and of course, silently.

When they reached the intersection, they cracked the wall door open and saw the Grand Gallery bustling with soldiers and medical personnel. Robert and Mark looked at each other, then simply walked out and joined the stream of soldiers flowing down the grand staircase and out.

Nobody paid them any attention, they were part of the stream of people rushing out. There were soldiers flanking the stream, weapons up, forming an armed guard, and soldiers on the floor dismantling the explosives. Robert had explained that they'd found what they thought were all the detonators and at any rate, there was a radio jammer throughout the Louvre calibrated to the frequency of the detonators.

They stepped outside.

Harper stopped when, far in the distance, she saw the black hole where the glorious golden Pyramid had been. Her heart broke, just a little, and she hoped they'd rebuild it as soon as possible. Big spotlights were up in the inner courtyard and the shards of glass glittered in the harsh light.

"We'll rebuild," Robert murmured, and Mark nodded.

"Damn right."

Harper wrenched her attention away from the ruins of the Pyramid and could see at the entrance to the huge square a series of trucks with antennas on top. Bright lights shone on news anchors from all over the world.

A teeming tide of people was held back by the police.

"Come," Robert said, and they walked away from the courtyard, the ruins, the people. "We must get you out another way."

They descended into what was once the entrance to the Louvre under the Pyramid, down the still escalator, right into a series of corridors with temporary exhibits, then through a door into a concrete stairwell and down several floors. Then a long dusty corridor, lit only by the two men's flashlights, to another door. Up two flights, another corridor, then a fire door and...out. Back into the fresh air.

Harper took off the ski mask and gulped the air gratefully. The night smelled of the distant traffic she could hear but not see and the bushes lining a walkway.

Robert gestured and an unmarked vehicle with deeply tinted windows rolled silently up. Robert opened the door and Harper slid in. Mark stood for a moment, one hand on the roof of the vehicle, one hand on the door.

"You've got a mole in the police," Mark reminded Robert.

Robert's face turned grim. "Yes, we know. We'll find him or them, have no fear."

Mark nodded. "I can count on you and your office to keep us out of it." It wasn't a question, it was a statement.

"*Mais certainement,*" Robert replied. "And I understand your reasons."

Mark dipped his head to enter the back seat where she waited for him, but Robert put his hand on Mark's arm.

"Very few people know what you did here tonight, but *I* know. You saved the lives of hundreds of people and you saved the Louvre. We discovered enough C-4 to destroy the building a hundred times over. The French people owe you an enormous debt of gratitude."

Mark shook his head.

"No one knows, and no one *will* know, but your company will have top-level French business till the end of time, count on it. I have ways to make sure your company's name is always at the top of the list, and I ensure you I will do just that."

Mark gave a half smile, shook Robert's hand and finally joined her in the back seat.

He put his arm around her, pulled her toward him for a chaste kiss on the forehead and met the driver's eyes in the rearview mirror.

"The Ritz, *s'il vous plaît.*"

13

There was something she had to understand, right now, his warrior princess. Mark watched her in the intermittent light of the tall ornate streetlamps. She'd been through hell. It was a miracle they were alive. He could still see the marks of the gas mask on her delicate skin.

And yet she was more beautiful than ever, classy and smart and *alive!* They'd come through an ordeal few people would have survived. Harper had never been in battle before and she'd come through like...well, like Daenerys, the Mother of Dragons.

He bent his head toward her, drinking her in. Smelling her, feeling her, this woman who'd become *his* woman so quickly. And he knew there was no going back. She was the one for him. He'd thought that kind of thing was crap. Lots of attractive women in the world, he'd always thought. He'd bedded his fair share of them, but none had ever gotten under his skin like Harper.

He wanted a long, long time with her. The rest of his life, in fact. But they had to be alive to do that. If they had any shot at spending their lives together, she had to understand one thing, and she had to understand it deep in her bones, in every cell of her body, with both her head and her heart.

Mark gently took Harper's chin with his thumb and forefinger and turned her head toward him. She'd been looking out the window at the glory of Paris along the Seine. Except for the dark shadow of the Louvre—unlit but still there—the buildings along the river were lit with a golden light, stunning, spectacular.

If not for the looming dark structure now behind them, there'd be no sign of the violence and terror of the past hours.

"Harper," he said softly, "listen to me. This is very important."

Her eyes sharpened and he could almost feel her focus. "Yes?"

"We just survived the biggest terror attack since 9/11. And we had a big hand in stopping it. Do you understand?"

She nodded, huge eyes fixed on his face. "Yes, of course."

"It is—would be—the biggest media story of the year. Maybe the decade. We'd be famous. You'd write a book. It would definitely get made into a movie."

Mark was relieved to see that the idea didn't enthuse her. Most people would have started counting the money in their head, eyes going ka-ching! But her eyes remained cool, focused on him. On what he was saying. It felt like she was listening to him through her skin and eyes and bones, not just through her ears.

"You could write your own ticket, your magazine would have advertisers coming out of its ears, you'd be on TV."

Mark himself would never be on TV. His work was in the shadows and he wanted it to stay that way. But he was different, he knew. Most people would kill to be on TV, become famous.

But...

"But you might not live long enough to enjoy your wealth and fame."

Her eyes widened.

"You'd be painting a bullseye right on your back." Mark took her hands in his. They were soft and cold and trembled slightly. He was frightening her but it was also the effects of adrenaline. "That attack was probably years in the planning. Embedding that many officers in the French police force would have taken time and immense effort. It was planned and timed, which meant they rehearsed it over and over. If it had succeeded, it would have been a world-changing event. But they were thwarted and if they discover they were thwarted by two people, they'll come after us with all they've got. It's the only way they can save face."

He held her hands more tightly. "Robert went to a lot of trouble to keep us out of it. He's going to wipe down the inside handle of the door and the butt of the gun you used to whack the lead terrorist."

She made a distressed sound in the back of her throat, and he bent to kiss her quickly on the lips.

"I'm really glad you did, honey. You saved my life. And now I'm doing my damnedest to save yours. So, do you understand me? No one must ever know we were there and that we did what we did. Ever. Not your mother and father, not your best friend. No one must know. I can't stress that enough. Are you with me on this?"

He could see the headlines. *Shadowy Billionaire Assassinated in Terrorist Ambush. Young Woman Who Helped Stop the Louvre Attack Shot Down.*

The car came to a stop in front of the Ritz, but Mark kept a tight hold on her hand and made no move to get out.

"Harper? Do you understand? Our lives depend on our silence."

Her face tightened, pale eyes gleaming in the darkness of the limo.

"Yes," she said finally. "I understand completely. No one can ever know what we did tonight."

"No one," Mark repeated. "No one at all. Not even a hint." He was being annoying but goddamn, this was important. It was all too easy to see her dead body, shot in the head, the killer with the sniper rifle calmly putting the pieces of the rifle back in its case, feeling nothing and not caring that he'd just put an end to Mark's world.

Harper freed a hand and stroked his face with her fingertips. A small gesture but it touched something deep inside him.

"Rest easy," she said softly. "I'd hate a media circus even if it didn't put us in danger. No one will ever know."

Nail it down, he thought.

"Not your best friend since grade school, not your sister, not your brother, not your parents or grandparents."

The fingers tracked down to his chin. She cupped it, in a gesture he was beginning to be familiar with.

"My best friend since grade school is a major gossip, I don't have siblings, my grandparents are dead, and I wouldn't dare tell my parents because they'd have heart attacks. They get upset when I fly, let alone take down terrorist attacks. I would never, ever tell them what happened. I wouldn't dare."

He searched her eyes and encountered only calm certainty.

"Okay, then."

The driver had rounded the car and held open the back door. Mark got out and held out his hand for her.

She stepped out like a queen. Her clothes were dirty and dusty but she held herself like royalty. She dusted herself off and straightened her clothes and you'd have to look carefully to see anything out of the ordinary. He, on the other hand, looked like he'd just come in from the wars.

Of course, in a way, he had.

They held hands as they walked across the sumptuous

lobby. Mark had the room cardkey in his pocket but decided to veer to the front desk, make contact with the concierge.

"I'd like you to send two *steak frites* up to my suite in an hour," he said.

Even the super-polite and well-trained concierge's eyes rounded at that. "But—but *monsieur*," he sputtered. "It's six o'clock in the morning."

Then he pursed his lips. It was not his place to criticize clients. And everyone knew that Americans were barbarians.

"I know." Mark smiled down into Harper's eyes. "But we've been out of town and we're hungry. I'd like my steak rare. You?"

"*Bleu aussi*," she said to the concierge. Mark knew that *bleu* meant bloody.

"*Oui, monsieur.*" The concierge tapped on a screen on the desk. "Have you heard the news, *M'sieur, madame*?"

Mark and Harper stood smiling into each other's eyes, seemingly lost to the world.

Harper was the first to answer. "Hmmm?" She turned her gaze from Mark with an almost audible wrench. "What news?"

"The hostages have been freed!" The concierge beamed.

Harper looked utterly blank as she stared at the concierge. "Hostages? What hostages?"

Under that cosmopolitan veneer, the concierge was shocked. "The hostage situation at the Louvre, *madame*. Terrorists attacked the *Louvre!*"

His outrage was clear.

Harper's eyes rounded. "The Louvre? The *Louvre* was attacked?" She covered her mouth in shock. The very picture of consternation.

Clearly, Mark wasn't needed here. He stood back a little and watched a master at work, falling a little more in love with every second. She lied like a pro. He really admired that.

"Yes." The concierge's thin lips pursed again. "Terrorists overran the Louvre, killed many tourists and took a hundred

tourists hostage in the room with the *Mona Lisa.*
They *slashed* the *Mona Lisa.* They threatened to blow up the
Louvre, destroy it." He stopped, breathing heavily.

"Oh my God," Harper whispered. "And what happened?"

The concierge straightened. "And then the French police
attacked them and freed all the hostages. They are all alive and
all the terrorists have been captured."

Interesting, Mark thought, that the police were getting the
credit. Maybe it would be straightened out later. He didn't care
either way. And those in the know would be congratulating
Robert.

The concierge narrowed his eyes. "You haven't heard
anything about this? It's been all over the media."

"Oh. Well." Harper leaned against him. Mark didn't know
how she did it, but she brought up a pretty little blush from
somewhere. "We've been away and…busy."

She didn't have to say it, it was implicit. They'd been
fucking like bunnies somewhere isolated.

And bam!

The image of the two of them in bed, having sex, filled his
brain. Filled his nostrils, filled his lungs, filled his dick with
blood.

The entire night at the Louvre was almost forgotten, a dim
memory, because right now all he could think about was
Harper and getting her into his room and getting into her, as
fast as he could.

If he could have pushed a button to send them straight to
his bedroom, naked, him already inside her, he would have.

And right there, in the Ritz's famous elegant lobby, with a
snobby concierge in front of him, he was hard as a rock and
nowhere to go with it.

And he was about ready to blow, with Harper right there by
his side, touching him, looking at him out of the corner of her

eye, smiling slightly. For the first time since he was fourteen, he was about ready to come in his pants.

Combat hard-on, surely. But also because he wanted Harper right now with a ferocity that surprised him.

They had to get away. Like, *now*.

Harper was listening with apparent fascination to the concierge's account of the attack on the Louvre, making appropriate *oh* sounds with that delectable mouth of hers. He pulled at her elbow, startling her.

"We have to go. Now." His voice was hard, as hard as his dick. She could see the state he was in, though luckily the concierge couldn't see below his waist over the counter.

Mark pulled her toward the elevators. While walking, she half turned and waved at the concierge. Mark didn't turn around to do the same, not with that tent in his pants.

Luckily, the elevator was waiting for them on the ground floor. Mark ushered Harper in with a hand to her back, then stabbed the button for his floor as if it were his own personal enemy.

They stood stiffly in the elevator, staring straight ahead, watching each other's reflections in the burnished copper plates of the inside doors.

He had his arm around her waist, and couldn't let go, not for anything. "Can't kiss you," he said, his voice guttural.

She'd picked up on it, on the fact that he was like a bag of C-4, just waiting to detonate.

She shook her head.

"Couldn't stop."

She nodded her head.

The fates were kind and delivered them quickly to his floor. He showed enormous self-control because he didn't pick her up and carry her to his door. The security cameras were no doubt showing a normal couple, walking normally, though if the cameras had infrared capability, he would have shown up as incandescent red, like a star about to go nova.

The corridor, the door, the card key...his vision tunneled, the world reduced to the next barrier on the way to bed.

Finally, they were in the bedroom and then on the bed, because he was about ready to explode.

He ripped off his jacket, pulled off the shirt, undershirt, unzipped his pants, shucked his boots and socks off, pulled pants and briefs down. All the while kissing her wildly. He wanted to hold her head while he kissed but he only had two hands. He should have had six hands—two to hold her head, two to get naked, two to get *her* naked. Eight hands—two more to hold her hips.

But he only had two. And those two were now getting rid of her clothes, which was a little hard because she was lying on her back and he was on top of her.

He was a good mission planner, known for strategic thinking. But that had gone. At this moment he only knew the straight line between now and when he could enter her.

He pulled her up, got rid of everything up top, shifted to the side of her, and got rid of everything on the bottom and then, ah...there they were. Naked.

He shifted back on top of her and spread her legs with his thighs, poised at her entrance, feeling the warm wetness between her legs.

Mark lifted his head, looking at her light gray eyes and swollen mouth. "No time for foreplay," he whispered regretfully.

Harper smiled, eyes nearly closed. "No need. Turns out thwarting terrorists is a massive turn-on. Who knew?"

And she wrapped her thighs around his, moving her hips forward, and he slid right into her. She was right—she *was* massively turned on.

God, so was he.

Holding her head, kissing her endlessly, he gave two hard thrusts and it was over. He exploded inside her, thrusting wildly...sharp, short, hard movements, totally out of his control. In the end, he held himself as deeply inside her as possible while being wrung dry.

It was mindless, exhilarating, white-hot pleasure—and embarrassing once it was over. He let go of her mouth, braced on his forearms, head hanging down between his shoulders, concentrating on his dick inside her. His entire body was drowning in pleasure, like all his skin was coming too.

He stayed inside her for a time out of time, could have been minutes, could have been hours, could have been *days*. He had no way of knowing, all he could pay attention to was the orgasm that had come screaming out of his dick by way of his head and his toes and everything in between.

He shook, trembled, sweated, hanging over her, panting. Coming and coming.

When he came back into himself, he was drowning in honeyed pleasure while ashamed. His toes were dug into the mattress to push himself as far as possible in her. He had really strong hands and they were clutching the sides of her head. Was he hurting her?

He softened his grip immediately. God, the thought of hurting her...

This was a woman he'd fallen in love with, a woman of grace and class, and he'd mounted her like a rutting warthog. He breathed in deeply. He smelled like a rutting warthog, too. Their groins smelled of sex and they were both wet.

He was going to have to apologize, though probably apologizing meant pulling out of her and he didn't know if he could do that. Not right now, anyway. His dick didn't want to go anywhere.

But he had to do something. Maybe just saying *I'm sorry* might be enough. Without actually pulling out.

On a sigh, Mark opened his eyes, perfectly prepared to find an angry face under him. What he found was a tense face, as if she were straining for something...

And her soft, wet sheath all of a sudden gripped him intensely, pulsing around him, and her head fell back against the mattress, exposing that long, slender, elegant neck, and she moaned and came, holding him tightly with her arms and legs.

It lasted a long time. She writhed around him, moaning his name, and the hairs on the back of his neck stood up and he got goose bumps just watching her. She was so beautiful, basking in her pleasure that was a pure gift from the gods of sex. He'd had nothing to do with it—he'd pursued his own pleasure mindlessly. The fact that she got off was a miracle, and it was no thanks to him.

Mark simply held her as she contracted around him, rubbing against him like a cat, enjoying the hell out of it.

When she finally subsided on one last long sigh that ruffled his hair, he held her tightly. His own miracle.

"We need to do that more often," he whispered in her ear.

Harper sighed again. "If we do, I won't survive a year."

They laughed, their bellies meeting. Mark sobered, looking down at her. This woman who in such a short span of time had become so precious to him.

He was suddenly seized with a burning desire to take care of her.

He kissed the tip of her nose, pulled out of her reluctantly, his dick complaining bitterly. It liked staying exactly where it was—deep inside her, where it was warm and soft.

He opened his mouth to offer to wash her back in the shower—and that image made his dick stir—when she gave his chest a sharp push.

He lifted himself off her, though it was hard renouncing all that soft warmth.

"I need to shower," Harper announced. She looked him severely in the eyes. "*Alone.*"

Fuck. There went the fantasy of washing her back, washing her lower body...

"I'm beginning to recognize that look in your eyes, and I am not up for another round until I have a shower and I eat." She nodded sharply, then smiled. "But once I'm clean and have eaten..."

She leaped out of bed laughing and ran to the bathroom.

Well. Mark had caught himself a live one. With a mind of her own and no hesitation in speaking it.

He wouldn't have it any other way.

The shower started up and Mark could just picture her slipping under the water, beautiful face turned up to the shower-head, the water running down her body in rivulets. He sighed. He'd given himself a hard-on, just thinking of it.

He wavered. She'd said no, but *man* he'd like to join her in the shower. Suds her up, his hands sliding over her sleek form, reaching down between her legs, where she'd be hot and wet—

The doorbell rang. Fuck, who on earth could it be?

"*Service à l'étage,*" a voice called out. Room service. Steak and French fries. Oh yeah. His stomach growled fiercely, annoyed at having been forgotten. It felt like he hadn't eaten for months.

The waiter entered and with a minimum of fuss, set up a table for them. He left the serving cart there, two plates covered with silver domes, which did nothing to hide the amazing smells coming from under them. He'd even opened a bottle of Bordeaux early morning. Mark figured he and Harper probably fell under the heading of crazy Americans.

Fine.

The thick linen napkins came with a napkin holder decorated with crystal beads forming a flower. Hmmm.

Mark reached for his Leatherman, took out needle-nosed pliers and bent to the task.

Just as he finished, the bathroom door opened and Harper came out in a rush of billowing steam, like clouds. The hotel bathrobe engulfed her but Mark knew intimately what was beneath it. She'd washed her hair and it fell in damp shiny waves to her shoulders. She was somehow even more beautiful without makeup, with a slight flush under the ivory skin, the elegant planes of her face even more evident.

She stopped, eyes wide, and sniffed the air. "Good God, is that *food* I smell?" Her eyes fell on the cart and she rushed forward—until Mark snagged his arm around her waist and pulled her against him.

"I have something to say to you."

She laughed and pushed at his shoulder. "Whatever it is, it can't be as important as food. Gimme."

He sighed heavily. "And here I was thinking you looked like a beautiful angel coming out of the bathroom." He shook his head sorrowfully. "And all you're thinking about is food."

She wriggled in his grasp, but he wasn't letting her go. "Damn right. Keeping me from that food is not a smart move, mister."

He turned her around, kissed her nose, and fell to one knee.

Her face took on a comical look of astonishment, luscious mouth shaping an O. "What are you doing?"

"What does it look like I'm doing? If you can take your mind off your stomach for just a second, I'm trying to propose here."

She just blinked at him.

Mark wiped the grin off his face. This next part was serious stuff and he needed a serious answer.

"Harper Kendall. I haven't known you long but I've seen you in the worst circumstances possible, and I like what I see. I love you, and you can believe it or not, but I've never said those words to any woman. We can have as long an engagement as you like but at the end of it, I hope you'll do me the honor of becoming my wife."

He took her hand, kissed it, and slipped the improvised engagement ring he'd made from the napkin ring onto her finger. They both stared down at the huge crystal flower wobbling on her finger.

He looked up into her eyes. Suddenly, his heart was pounding and he could feel sweat trickling down his back. He was known for his cool on the battlefield, but right now he was very close to panic. "Well?"

She looked at him, eyes flashing from side to side as she studied his face. Her fingers toyed with the ring.

He was holding his breath without realizing it, because when she said, "Yes," he had to gulp in air.

"That was a yes," he said, his voice hoarse.

"It was." She nodded, smiling.

"Yes to everything. Marriage, kids, everything."

"Yes," she whispered, and leaned forward to kiss him gently on the mouth. "To everything."

The world wobbled then straightened and he felt certainty settle in him. He looked down at the ridiculous ring.

"We'll go shopping for a real ring this afternoon. I'm told there's a good jewelry shop down the road. You might have heard of it. Shop called Cartier. Where I'll buy you a diamond as big as the Ritz."

PREVIEWS

Dear Reader, I hope you enjoyed **CHARADE Her Billionaire – Paris**. If you did, you might also enjoy **MASQUERADE Her Billionaire – Venice** and **ESCAPADE Her Billionaire – London** two more sexy, sophisticated stories. Here are the first chapters of MASQUERADE and ESCAPADE:

1

MASQUERADE PREVIEW
BOSTON, TEN YEARS AGO

Calvin Burns stroked the beautiful back of the woman he loved, Anya Voronova. It was snowing outside his miserable, shabby dump of a studio apartment, the white mantle covering the overfilled dumpsters, filling in the cracks in the sidewalk, softening the smell of rot and mold.

But inside his room was magic. He didn't see the sagging bed, plyboard desk, scratched appliances. With Anya in the room, it was like being in a palace housing the rarest of treasures. Her naked body on his cheap rumpled bed glowed like the finest ivory. Her long blonde hair rippled down her back, gleaming gold.

Fuck, *listen to him.*

Cal was an engineer. Engineers were bound by facts and equations and hard cold math. If his profs or students in the post grad engineering classes he taught could read his mind right now, they'd freak. Cal Burns did math. Cal Burns didn't do poetic.

But then, nobody else had Anya Voronova as a lover. She'd inspire a gorilla to poetry. She was like winning the lottery and discovering the cure for cancer and inventing computers all wrapped up in one winning package.

He tapped out *We are the Champions* on her satiny back, right above the dimple over her perfect ass.

"Mmm." She made a throaty sound of pleasure.

"Like that, do you?" Cal asked. He didn't have to ask. Anya always made her pleasure — and displeasure — known. She didn't play games. He loved that about her.

But then, he loved everything about her.

She smiled at him over her shoulder, light blue eyes gleaming. "Do you know who used to do that?"

Cal froze. "Do what?" Was she going to talk about some lover she'd had before him who'd touched that perfect back? Jealousy shot through him in a spurt of bile.

"Tapping something rhythmic on the back of a woman. Goethe did that, tapping out the hexameters of one of his poems on his lover's back. In his palazzo in Rome."

Goethe. Cal had only discovered who Goethe was since he'd started dating Anya and the first time he saw the name written he would have pronounced it Go-thee. Luckily she pronounced it out loud first. Ghew-tay.

And fuck if he knew what a hexameter was.

Another thing about this beautiful woman. She was cultivated as hell, knew everything there was to know about non-scientific, non-engineering things. Cal more or less had the scientific, engineering side of things down pat, so together they were going to rule the world.

"Well." Cal sighed, smoothing the palm of his hand over the satiny skin of Anya's lower back. "Not a poet. Couldn't write a poem to save my life."

She chuckled and slowly turned over. Every time Cal met those bright summer-sky blue eyes, it was like a punch to the stomach. She was so beautiful she took his breath away.

He hadn't moved his hand but her turning over placed his

hand on her stomach. It wasn't a hardship. That very soft skin covered sleek firm muscles all over. She smiled right into his eyes, placing her hand over his, pushing it down.

"I don't know, darling," she whispered. "In some things you're an artist."

And she moved her long slim legs apart and the hard punch of lust nearly brought him to his knees. She smiled. She knew exactly what she did to him.

One leg bent, one long leg open to the side and there she was — open to him. They'd made love not long ago and she was still pink and swollen there. Glistening from her juices. Cal remembered vividly shaking as he came and jetted what felt like half his bodily fluids into the condom and feeling how wet she was when he pulled out.

Her sex was a living embodiment of their love-making, like she'd been branded. He liked that, liked the thought of her being branded by him. Her sex, her breasts ... the nipples were still hard and deep pink from his mouth. There was a little whisker burn on the ivory skin of her breasts which he'd feel sorry for if he hadn't loved sucking on her nipples so much. She hadn't complained.

In a deeper way, he was branded, too. Highly sexed by nature, Cal now thought of sex exclusively in terms of Anya. No one else turned him on at all. He couldn't even consider having another woman, not when he had the most beautiful woman in the world in his bed, who was also whip smart and understood him.

And loved him.

That was the real kicker. She loved him.

"Cal," she breathed, and all the hairs on his body stood up. He was already hard as a rock. He was always semi-aroused when around her. But when they were naked together, his dick simply wouldn't go down.

"Honey." There was a slight question in the word. What did

she want? Whatever she wanted, he'd give to her. He'd give her the moon if he could.

Her huge, bright blue eyes locked onto his face. "Touch me."

Cal shuddered. God, yes. He reached out and gently pushed her legs further apart. The skin of her inner thighs felt warm and incredibly soft against the skin of his palm. His hands were big and rough. He'd been into martial arts since he was a kid and had had a karate period. He had tough, calloused hands. But he knew from experience that no matter how rough his hands were, they didn't scratch her skin. He knew exactly how to touch her, where and how hard.

"That's it," Anya whispered as his hand rose along her thigh, higher and higher.

Cal sat on the side of the bed and just looked at her, stretched out before him like a feast, legs apart, eyes heavy.

There was some painter from some time in the past who'd painted this painting ... he didn't remember the name of the artist, or the style or the name of the painting. That wasn't in his wheelhouse, though it was in hers. She was the one who'd showed him the image in a book.

All he remembered was skin that glowed like pearls on the canvas, the woman looking straight at the viewer, long blonde hair covering part of her body, one hand on her belly. It was a famous painting and if his mind hadn't been blasted by lust maybe he'd remember what it was called, but he did remember the beauty of the model that seared the eyes.

That was what Anya looked like, only she was more slender and her hair was honey blonde not red. But other than that, she was eternal woman.

Cal shifted his eyes to her belly, where his hand lay next to hers. Just the sight of their hands together was erotic, let alone how she was posed. His hands were big and callused from years at the dojo. He could shatter four bricks with the edge of his hand but here it looked out of place against her delicate skin. Her hand was slender and pale, the hand of an artist. Male and female.

He slid his hand further down and covered her mound, like a flesh-colored bikini bottom. She had a cloud of ash-brown hair covering her sex, it was so soft to the touch it felt like a cloud too. Small dots of her juices were threaded through her pubic hair like tiny pearls.

She smiled at him, meeting his eyes, then hers travelled over his body down to his groin, where he was as hard as a club. He felt more blood rush to his dick. It was almost painful.

She smiled up into his eyes. "Just from looking at you?"

"Just you breathing does the trick, princess."

She rolled her eyes, as she always did when he called her princess. But the fact was, she *was* a princess, sort of. Her asshole father, who was insanely rich, never failed to mention in interviews that he was descended from Russian royalty. His great-great- a billion times great-grandfather had been a cousin of the czar a million years ago when Russia had czars. It was in every interview with the man. Anya never mentioned it but her father did. Often.

He was a dickhead. Cal hated him and he hated Cal right back.

Not that Cal cared. Not when he had his princess looking at him with heat in her glowing blue eyes.

She lifted her leg and placed her foot right over his dick. Cal closed his eyes because it was just too much stimulation. Her foot was beautiful too, slender, pretty, with blue toenail polish. She rubbed it up and down him and his breathing went ragged.

He had to do something to even this up.

Cal turned his hand, started stroking her. He heard a sharp intake of breath and opened his eyes to see her closing hers. Fuck yeah. He wasn't alone here. She was wet and pink and slightly swollen, from the last time they'd made love and from her body preparing for the next time.

He watched as his hand stroked her, the wet skin like satin. A finger traced her opening, around and around, lingering at the clitoris. He knew her so well. Her excitement was so fascinating he almost forgot his own.

Around and around ... her thighs trembled.

Yeah, baby.

He slipped his finger inside her, relishing the small cry. She convulsed around his finger sharply and he could see her stomach muscles pull. When his princess came, she came with her whole body.

She wasn't quite there yet, though. Close, but not there.

"Cal ..." Anya whispered.

He leaned down, one hand planted on the bed right next to her pale firm breast. "Sweetheart." He pulled his finger out, slid it back in. She convulsed again, a sharp pull of her sex. Her hands were trembling.

His were, too.

"Come to me," she pleaded and it wasn't in him to deny her. Of course he would come to her. He was born to come to her.

He slid a second finger into her silky warmth, holding her open, placed a knee on the bed and mounted her, sliding into her in the exact moment she started coming.

Oh my god, she was so beautiful when she came. He never got tired of it. He wanted to spend the rest of his life watching her. There was a ring in his pants pocket with a tiny diamond in it. So tiny you could hardly see it, but the promise behind the ring was big. He was hers, forever.

She was arched back, long neck exposed. He lowered his mouth to her neck and as his lips touched her skin, she came even harder, pulsing against his dick. There was an electrical connection that nearly stopped his heart.

He pressed inside her, mouth on her neck, feeling the fluttering of her heart. His own heart was thundering inside his chest, with excitement, with love.

Man, he loved her. He didn't think it was possible to love any human being as much as he loved Anya Voronova, his princess. He felt her skin against his, but it was like her skin had been removed and he could feel her insides, too. Her heart beating, her muscles pulling, her lungs expanding. He was inside her and she was inside him.

It was exhilarating and a little scary too.

But, hell, worth it.

Cal held himself still while she worked her way through her orgasm, hyperaware of everything going on with her. Her sex clenching around his, her arms and legs holding him tightly, the way she arched her back and stopped breathing for a long moment, as she went inside herself, completely in the moment.

Then she crested, a sharp moan coming from her, her hips rotating, almost dancing around his dick while coming. He let her because it was a way for her body to be prepared.

Cal could be rough. He didn't want to be, particularly not with his princess, but it was the way he was wired. The only way it could work was if she came and came hard and was soft and wet afterward. So he gritted his teeth as she climaxed, then came down gently, her entire body lax and mellow. Arms and legs falling back onto the mattress, wet and soft inside.

Now he could let loose.

Cal lowered his entire body onto her and buried his face in the pillow next to hers. In his excitement he didn't want to mark her, even – God forbid! – bite her. In the early days he'd been so worked up he marked that perfect ivory skin a couple of times and it had appalled him.

He slid his hands up her slim legs and lifted them and opened them a little, so that — ah — he reached deep inside her. If he could, he'd have touched her heart with his dick. As it was, he did his best.

And then all thoughts fled his head as he became a male animal with his mate.

He retained just enough control not to pound her, but it was hard. Every single cell in his body registered acute mind-numbing pleasure as he moved in and out of her, fast then faster. She was soft and warm and all his. Skin to skin, heart to heart, on her and in her, he moved, heart pounding, barely registering pleasure when she convulsed and came again. Her arms held him so tightly, but not as tightly as he held her. He wanted to stay inside her forever but when her hands moved to his butt and her fingers curled in and she nipped his earlobe — he lost it.

Cal moved as fast and as hard as he could, feeling her pleasure, feeling that he wasn't hurting her but pleasing her, but it was way too much. Too much stimulation — that soft, creamy skin, that luscious mouth kissing his ear, her soft, wet sex like a glove around him ...

He erupted with a great groan, lungs bellowing because there wasn't enough air in the world to contrast the enormous heat inside him, like a volcano exploding, hips making short fast jabs inside her until it was over and he collapsed on top of her, completely spent.

His breathing gradually slowed down and he gained the use of his body back. Every time it was as if he entered some secret kingdom where he gave her so much power over him he had to work his way back into himself.

He did it this time, too. But this time, there was a reason for him to get back in control of himself. He had big news. Big *big* news. The biggest.

His face was still buried in the pillow next to hers and a huge grin broke out, one he couldn't control. He let it bloom because ... *hot damn*. His life — their lives — were about to change.

It was supposed to be a surprise because it was so big he'd

been afraid to blow the possibility of it out of proportion with her. They'd barely talked about it because he didn't want to jinx it and he didn't want to see disappointment in her eyes if he didn't get it.

Already the difference in status between them was huge, an almost unbridgeable gap. But he was an engineer and his love for her had built the bridge between them, which existed only when they were in their little world of two. And here, in his slum of a flat. He'd been to her palatial mansion only once and the memory was so painful he winced every time he thought of it.

She was the daughter of an immensely rich aristocrat and he was the son of a runaway mom and a drunk truck driver of a father, who'd cut off relations when Cal wanted to go to college instead of driving a truck like his dad.

But all of that was going to change. Something big was coming up and he had a ring with a microscopic diamond in his pocket for when he'd given his news and he could officially ask her to marry him. He'd have asked the day after meeting her but he'd had nothing to offer.

He did now.

Like in a fairy tale, he and his princess would move and begin their lives together in a beautiful sunny kingdom far far away.

California.

She was working on a double major — Chinese studies and International Relations. She could do that just as well at Berkley as here. Better.

She'd come with him.

But first — he had to tell her his news.

Cal lifted his head then his torso up on his forearms. He kissed her forehead, pulled gently out of her. His dick complained, just like it always did because inside Anya was the best place to be. His dick hated pulling out.

But his dick could take a hike because there was serious stuff to talk about now.

"I have some news," he said softly, trying to keep the excitement out of his voice. Time for excitement later.

Anya pushed gently at his chest, their sign for him to get off her. When they were having sex, she said his weight on her was exciting. But he weighed almost double what she did and she always said that breathing was overrated when they were having sex, but became once again a priority post-sex.

Obediently, Cal rolled off her and she scooted up to sit against the plywood headboard, bunching pillows around her.

Oh man. She was just so beautiful sitting there, a naked princess with flat cheap pillows around her for a throne.

"So." She smiled at him. "What's the news? Is Kreizler going to let your name be on the paper?"

Cal frowned. Fuck, he'd forgotten about that. He'd done most of the work on a big paper on the elastic properties of graphene, staying up nights at the lab, laboriously recording tension and yield test results. Kreizler had made a half-assed promise that Cal's name would go on the paper but Cal had just seen the program for the World Conference of Materials Science to be held next March in Dublin and, nope. His name wasn't on the paper.

But that didn't make any difference now. He was going to leave Kreizler in the fucking dust. Leapfrog right over the bastard who treated him like hired help.

"Nah. He's not sharing. Didn't even have the nerve to tell me himself, I found out by checking the paper online. But, who the fuck cares?" He picked up her hand, soft and slender, and brought it to his mouth. "Because something better is on the horizon." He tried to control his breathing. "I got it. Anya, *I got it.*"

He was trying to keep the excitement down but his voice turned hoarse. He cleared his throat.

She took her other hand and smoothed away a lock of his too long hair. Damn, his hair grew out so fast and he didn't have the money to keep going to the barber. She smoothed the lock of hair behind his ear, still smiling gently at him. "Got what, darling?"

He was looking deep into her eyes but he closed his. He didn't want to watch her face when he told her the news because then ... well if she teared up then so would he and if he started crying the Man Police would rip his Y chromosome right out of him.

He swallowed heavily, held her hand tightly. "I got that post-doc fellowship at Stanford. Working with a top-tier research team headed by Habericht, who has a Nobel, and by Loren, who won a McArthur Genius Award three years ago. And that's not all. I got an offer from Benson Labs for a part time job that will become a full-time job after the fellowship. And the salary from Benson Labs will pay off my student loans in the first year."

He gave a sigh that came from deep in his chest. He was drowning in student debt.

This was like a dream come true. Cal smiled, opened his eyes — and froze.

Anya's lovely face was utterly blank. Not warm and welcoming, not happy for him, not anything. Just blank and ... cold?

What the fuck?

"Anya, honey, I —" But he didn't know what to say. Because all of a sudden, he wasn't touching her anymore and he hadn't moved. She had. She'd moved ... away from him.

And, oh fuck, she was out of bed, bending to pick up her clothes on the floor.

What had he said? Had he thought he'd told her about Stanford but instead something else had come out of his mouth? Had he had a stroke or been struck by one of those weird syndromes where only profanities came out of his mouth?

Fuck, no.

He remembered precisely what he'd said. *I got it.* Which was supposed to be her cue to cry out with joy and hug him and maybe he'd get another round of sex before asking her to marry him.

That was the way it was supposed to go. So what was happening right now? Something bad was happening, that was what. And he was powerless to stop it.

His muscles were paralyzed as he watched her pick up her dainty, lacy underwear from the floor. She always dressed simply. Bra, underpants, sweater, yoga pants, socks, boots and finally parka.

Cal was too dumbfounded to stop her, ask what she was doing. That was pointless anyway because it wasn't hard to figure out what she was doing. She was leaving. Instead of spending the night the way he'd hoped, she was going home.

He had just enough money left on his card to order pizzas in and the plan was to snuggle up with her and watch some pirated movie on his ancient laptop. It hadn't even occurred to him that that was not the way he was going to be spending his evening, the way he'd spent so many evenings. With her.

But she wasn't staying.

As she laced her boots he shook off the frozen spell he was under.

"What are you doing?" His voice croaked, cracked.

"Seems clear what I'm doing." Her own voice was cool, controlled.

"You're *leaving?*" The idea was still so strange he had to hear it from her mouth.

"That's right, ace. I'm leaving." She zipped up her parka, flipped up the hood and turned to face him. She was like ice. It was warm in his room but a chill emanated from her.

It was so unfair that she was still so beautiful, even somehow angry at him. The hood of the parka was lined with dark fake fur that looked like the real thing. It framed her face like that of a princess in a fairy tale, the kind where the princess wandered into the dark forest and made the big bad wolf fall in love with her.

Her beautiful face was closed to him, eyes like shards of ice.

What the fuck? *What was happening?*

He was getting screwed, is what was happening to him. And not in a good way. A spurt of anger flashed and he repressed it immediately. He'd never gotten angry at Anya, ever. And he wasn't going to start now. He didn't want to start now.

But ... what the fuck?

After staring at him coldly for a long moment, Anya turned on her heel and walked to the door. Opened it. Walked out.

Hell.

Cal stared at the door stupidly. His muscles felt slow, his brain felt mired in mud. He couldn't react. He could barely breathe.

What just happened? Was there a pod in the lavish wine cellars of her father's mansion, eating the real Anya after extruding a fake alien? No, that had been the real Anya he'd made love to. Her skin, the sounds she made, the way she clutched at him ... those were all real.

Loving Anya was the best thing that ever happened to him. She loved him right back, he was sure of it. They were young but neither of them were dummies. They'd lucked into true love at a young age but they both realized what they had. It was rare and precious and needed protecting.

He loved her and she loved him. Or, up until five minutes ago, she'd loved him. Then something ... changed.

Misery was setting in, a dark cloud of it rising like some dank fog from the nether regions of the earth. From caves and crevices where dark creatures dwelled. His head ached. His bones ached.

Too late, he realized he should be chasing her. Cal moved forward, but slowly and painfully, like he'd just taken a bad beating at the dojo. He was good in the dojo, it had been years since anyone had been able to hurt him. But this felt like he'd been beaten to within an inch of his life.

He'd opened his door and was walking out before he realized that he was buck naked. Much as he wanted to, he couldn't chase her like this. They'd arrest him. So he went back in, pulled up his jeans over his hips, jerked on his shirt without buttoning it and jammed his sockless feet into his ancient running shoes.

He limped down the stairs as if both legs had been broken. Something in him was broken. He threw open the front door of his apartment building and stared out in dismay. As usual, the light over the door and every other street light was out. He never let Anya walk alone after dark in his area. The fact that she had ... he couldn't go there. The idea that she'd rather court danger than stay with him was so painful he batted the thought away instantly.

It was snowing hard. Not pretty snowflakes gently settling on the cracked ground, but frozen rain flooding from the sky. He could see her boot prints but they disappeared two feet from the door. Right was a long slog to the subway, left was a bus stop. But she'd have to change three buses to get home. She usually took the subway. But never alone after dark, ever.

Her boot prints went to the right. She'd opted for the subway, which — damn it! — was not safe. Neither the streets to get there nor the station itself.

He took off running. He was a martial artist, not a track star. Cal was powerful, but not a runner. Still, he made good time, following her footsteps until he couldn't any more, the thick falling snow smudging them out.

But he knew the way to the subway and he ran as fast as he could.

She wasn't there. Cal frantically searched the filthy, graffiti-painted station. There were a couple of drug addicts, an ancient alcoholic preaching the end of the world and some tired workers.

Cal stared at the dirty station through eyes that stung, one hand braced against the wall as if he would fall down any second as he anxiously screened every passenger. Even when the train clanked in and came to a screeching stop, he studied everyone who boarded and stalked up and down the platform, peering into every car. On the crazy chance that she'd ... what? Run two miles to the previous station and gotten on there?

Well clearly she hadn't headed for the subway. Maybe she'd doubled back. Probably she'd called a cab. He hadn't even thought of that, because cabs never entered into his calculations. He could probably build a rocket to fly him to the moon before he could cab it everywhere.

Finally, he trudged up the stairs and out into the freezing cold. Fishing his cell out of his jeans, he thumbed her number. It was the first on his contacts list. The call went to voice mail.

The call went to voice mail all night. He must have called a hundred times but he never left a message, not trusting his voice.

The next day he called, then went to her apartment. Her father had bought her a pretty little studio apartment in a nice part of town. He stood at the front door ringing her bell for an hour until the super came out and chased him away.

The super's name was Mac, or that was what Cal called him. He was Polish and his name had enough consonants to sound like a sneeze. Cal and Mac were friends. Cal had helped him with building repairs a lot of times. But Mac wouldn't look him in the eye and pretended that his English had deserted him.

Cal called the mansion, though the idea of accidentally catching Mr. Voronov scared him. No danger of that, though. The housekeeper always answered, assuring him in icy tones that Miss Anya was not there, no she didn't know where Miss Anya was or when Miss Anya was coming back and by the way don't bother calling again.

He sent emails, pouring out his heart. She couldn't hear the tears in his voice in an email. But the emails remained unopened and never answered. Three days later, when he called her cell he got an announcement that the number was no longer in use.

He lost ten pounds that first week and missed all his classes. When he almost missed the deadline for accepting the job with Benson Labs, Cal knew that his future was on the line.

He could obsess over Anya and mourn her or he could get his act together and move forward.

He faxed his acceptance and bought the ticket to San Francisco with the last of the money in his bank account

Ten days after Anya walked out on him, on a bitterly cold, sleety day, Cal packed his few belongings and flew out West, toward his future.

Without Anya.

Buy now!
Nook | iTunes | Kobo

2

ESCAPADE PREVIEW

CALVIN BYRNES BUILDING, MATHEMATICAL INSTITUTE, OXFORD

S he was a looker.

Really gorgeous in a punk schoolmarm-y kind of way. Not that any of the males in the room would notice. There was very little testosterone in this room of two hundred math geeks, most of them guys. More or less all the testosterone in the room was his, and it was sitting up and taking notice.

Not good.

Bennett Cameron wasn't used to having testosterone released during a job for anything but aggression. He was a close protection expert — a bodyguard, in civilian terms — and he was used to being alert to anything that could be a source of danger. When on the clock, his body was flooded with testosterone and cortisol, the arousal and stress hormones. Arousal as in all systems go, every sense up and running, including the sixth one.

Not arousal as in a hard-on.

He'd been a security consultant long enough to have a sixth and even seventh sense for danger. Nothing got by him.

Right now, nothing was pinging on his danger radar so all that testosterone went to one special part of his body, watching the lithe young beauty parade across the stage, mouthing mathematical formulae, following abstruse lines of thought, of which he understood one word in ten.

Still, he didn't have to understand her math. He just had to keep her safe.

But first he had to kidnap her.

That was a royal pain in the ass. And maybe not easy, either. Bennett watched her on the stage, pacing back and forth, elaborating some incredibly long and complicated thought that had the audience gasping, then tittering, then sighing. Whatever she was saying — and he had no hope of deciphering it — was a real hit with the geeks.

But where the geeks and nerds all looked lost, with their too big sweaters that looked like their moms had dressed them in expectation of that last spurt of growth, cumulatively smelling a bit rank, completely engrossed in what she was saying, the woman herself, Dr. Eleonore Castle, known by her peers as E. M. Castle for Eleonore Marion Castle, known by her friends as Elle, seemed very alert. Very aware of her surroundings. Those cobalt-blue eyes as she looked around the room seemed very very sharp.

She looked pretty unkidappable if he wanted to keep it calm and quiet.

He was at the back of the room, hiding behind a pillar. The stage lights were in her eyes. There was no chance that she could see him, but still he stuck to the shadows, biding his time. There was no way he could abduct her in front of two hundred geeks.

Well actually he *could* ... given the fitness level of the audience. But they would all surely have cellphones and a robust virtual life more interesting than their real lives, so the scene of Dr. Eleonore Castle being abducted in the civilized confines of the Mathematical Institute of Oxford University would explode and go viral on all social media in about five seconds.

Bennett's company operated below the radar, which is why it was so successful. A media frenzy would be bad for this op in particular and terrible for his company in general. Not to mention it would paint a huge bullseye on the good doctor's very pretty back, when he'd signed a million-dollar contract to protect that back. And front, for that matter.

Her talk was a long one but fascinating, to judge by the rapt expressions of the audience. Bennett himself didn't have a clue.

"And then one could just camp out on the x axis forever, am I right?" she said, bafflingly, and even more bafflingly, the whole room erupted in chuckles.

Well, he wasn't going to kidnap her in the auditorium, and what she was saying was nonsense to him, so he had best use the time in research. He was as good at research as he was in Close Quarters Combat and Close Protection, which was why his company had taken off.

Okay. Nothing like St. Google to give you info and ... oh wow. Pages and pages and *pages* of stuff on Dr. Castle. If you googled his name, Bennett Cameron, you'd get a few very spare returns and a tripwire in one of his back offices would send him a message that someone had pinged him. Bennett operated way under the radar.

But the people with the money to afford him knew about him and knew how to get in touch with him.

So, the very pretty doctor had academic credentials as long as his dick. A doctorate and two masters and a number of semi-nars that she both attended and taught. A list of publications that was impressive for someone so young, including two books. Wait — he didn't know how old she was. Her father hadn't told him. And she looked really young up there on the stage. And she had a doctorate and two masters and all those courses, so how the hell —

Oh. She went to Harvard when she was fourteen.

Damn.

A lot of brain power in that pretty head.

Bennett looked at what she'd been doing the past six months. Most people were creatures of habit and if you wanted to know where they were and what they were doing, your best bet was to check where they'd been and what they'd done.

Conferences all over the place, with strange names. Behavioral Economics, Mechanism Design, Circuits and Systems. Conferences in Berkley, Singapore, St. Petersburg, Las Vegas, Guangzhu, Abu Dhabi, just in the last six months alone. The woman got around.

This was not a bad thing. He could pass for a math nerd for about ten seconds and say they'd met at a conference. She couldn't possibly remember everyone she met when she was on the road so much.

So that was the play.

Catch her after the symposium, tell her they'd met in wherever, whenever, get her in a quiet space, explain about her father, whisk her away.

Done deal.

So Bennett waited patiently for her to finish her incomprehensible talk and tried not to let his mind wander. Someone in close protection never let their mind wander, ever. Intense vigilance while on the job was a prerequisite. Lose focus for a second and you could lose a life.

But right now, there was nothing to do and there was no imminent danger so he could relax his vigilance, just a bit.

He had a perfect view of the main entrance to the auditorium. There was a small hidden door behind the podium, too. Nobody could come in without him seeing who it was. If anything happened in the auditorium itself, if anyone stood up to shoot her, Bennett would shoot him first. He and his company worked often for the UK government and he had been granted a license to carry in the UK. He was an excellent shot. A former sniper, in fact.

So Bennett kept an eye on the beauty up on stage with a part of his head thinking in non-tactical terms.

Slender, long-limbed, agile. She paced gracefully as she unwound a long, involved line of reasoning that took up three slides of dense math on the screen. Bennett lost track immediately.

Man, she was just amazing. Particularly considering that her father, Clifford Ricks, resembled a toad. Eleonore or Elle or Ellie was the man's only child, fruit of his first marriage. The old man had gone on to five more marriages, each divorce costing him more than ten million dollars. Luckily, he had money to spare.

She was wearing a jacket that could only be described as post-modern. Cut askew, it was both weird and attractive because it hugged her slender curvy figure and it was a deep brilliant cobalt blue that exactly matched her eyes. And she was wearing tight, stovepipe black pants that exactly matched the color of her hair.

Bennett didn't often get a chance to admire who he was protecting, not in this way. He'd protected beautiful women before, usually the wives of rich men, their minds as empty as their faces were beautiful. Though, to tell the truth, he didn't do much close protection himself these days. He had men for that. A hundred and fifty of them, to be exact, all of them hand-picked.

It was a young man's game and though Bennett wasn't old, he wasn't young any more either. Too old for this kind of work. His company was moving into more intel-dense work, finding missing people, tracking down money launderers, that kind of thing.

He'd only accepted this contract because Clifford Ricks had begged him. Saying he'd get on his knees if he still could. Ricks's hedge fund had thrown millions of dollars' worth of work to Bennett's company and, well, a young woman in danger. It wasn't in him to refuse.

And now that he'd had a glimpse of the daughter, he was more glad than ever that he'd accepted the job.

Clifford Ricks's enemy was Anton Lipov, who headed an offshoot of the Volcic mob, known for its extreme cruelty. They placed their enemies on a meat hook and watched them die, over the course of days.

That wasn't going to happen to Elle Castle.

Whoa. The talk was over. Elle took a little sardonic bow as the auditorium rose, clapping.

Fuck. They all looked eager to rush to the podium to grab a bite of the star. Bennett couldn't protect her in a crowd, not without showing his hand and it was too early for that. He moved forward, running through scenarios in his head, when she suddenly ... disappeared.

What the hell?

The hidden door behind the podium clicked shut. She'd escaped out the back of the stage. Well, Bennett couldn't fault her. The smell of unwashed clothes and a few whiffs of major halitosis were detectable even at the back of the auditorium. He could only imagine how repulsive the nerds would be up close and personal. But now he was going to have to be fast to catch up with her.

He knew how to move fast without appearing to rush. He had long legs and he lengthened his stride without moving his upper body much. In a few seconds he was out the door and into the big hallway. The original building was ancient. He had no idea how ancient but it boasted spires and and flagstoned floors and stained glass windows. The math annexe was modern, though, with acres of carpeted hallways.

Bennett quartered the area without swiveling his head, without making it obvious he was looking for someone. There were three directions she could have gone and he studied each one carefully.

There! Making her way down the hallway which was the fastest route out of the building. And man, she was making tracks.

Bennett lengthened his stride even more. "Elle! Ellie! *Elle Castle!*" he called out behind her, relieved when she slowed and turned around.

"Hey!" Bennett put on his genial good guy face. He'd trained to kill since he was eighteen and he'd killed twelve men in battle and three in close protection. When he wanted to, he could switch to his war face and it was frightening. But he could also smile and look as harmless as someone built like him could look. He pasted a delighted smile on his face. "Good to see you! That was a really interesting talk back there."

Bennett wasn't a ladies' man, but he also wasn't bad looking and he knew how to charm the ladies when he had to. But Elle wasn't having it and was definitely not charmed. She stared up at him and it was like being caught in the beam of twin cobalt spotlights.

"Do I know you?" she asked, voice cold.

He plastered a hand over his heart. "You wound me, you really do. We shared a glass of indifferent champagne at the reception in St Petersburg. The caviar was good, though."

Her eyes searched his face. "No," she said flatly, "we didn't. I've never seen you before in my life."

Oh man. God save him from smart women with steel trap memories. She also seemed pretty impervious to his charms. Bennett took her arm gently, hoping to walk her closer to the exit door while trying to convince her they'd met before. He remembered the name of one of the authors of a paper.

"Surely you haven't forgotten Leontov too? And his dandruff?" Since the guy was a mathematician, it was a pretty good guess that he had dandruff. Unless he was completely bald. It was a 50-50 shot.

Eleonore Castle dug in her heels. To move her now he'd have to use at least a minimum amount of force. And she'd probably raise a fuss. They were surrounded by people. She looked pointedly at his hand on her elbow. "I'll thank you to stop manhandling me and to leave me alone, otherwise I'm calling security."

Well, she could hardly know that he'd easily deal with a Brit rent-a-cop. Or even several of them.

But they were wasting time on a very time-sensitive mission. Bennett stifled a sigh. He looked down into her beautiful angry mistrustful face and took an executive decision.

"Sorry, darling," he murmured. "I really don't want to do this, but I have to."

And he injected her with a fast-acting psychotropic drug that would make her amenable but not unconscious. She gave a small cry at the slight sting of the needle then, after a moment, her eyes unfocused.

Bennett waited a few seconds for the drug to take effect. He wasn't happy about it. He was a good guy and he was saving her life but man, he didn't like drugging a woman. But she was too smart for her own good, so what choice did he have?

"Come on, darling," he said and took her arm again.

She shambled forward obediently.

Get Masquerade!
Don't miss out on my other books!

ALSO BY LISA MARIE RICE

Men Of Midnight Series

Midnight Man

Midnight Run

Midnight Angel

Midnight Quest

Midnight Vengeance

Midnight Promises

Midnight Secrets

Midnight Fire

Midnight Fever

Midnight Renegade

Midnight Kiss

Midnight Embrace

Midnight Caress

Midnight Shadows

Her Billionaire Series

Charade

Masquerade

Escapade

Dangerous Passions

Reckless

Hot Secrets

ABOUT THE AUTHOR

Lisa Marie Rice is eternally 30 years old and will never age. She is tall and willowy and beautiful. Men drop at her feet like ripe pears. She has won every major book prize in the world. She is a black belt with advanced degrees in archaeology, nuclear physics, and Tibetan literature. She is a concert pianist. Did I mention her Nobel Prize?

Of course, Lisa Marie Rice is a virtual woman and exists only at the keyboard when writing romance. She disappears when the monitor winks off.

ABOUT THE AUTHOR